UNREMARKABLE

ISBN: 978-1-932926-49-1
LCCN: 2017909831

Copyright © 2018 by Geoff Habiger & Coy Kissee

Cover Design: Angella Cormier

Printed in the United States.

Shadow Dragon Press
9 Mockingbird Hill Rd
Tijeras, New Mexico 87059
www.shadowdragonpress.com
info@artemesiapublishing.com

Unremarkable

Geoff Habiger
&
Coy Kissee

Albuquerque, NM

Geoff and Coy dedicate this book to our moms (Connie, Linda, and Lynn) who encouraged our fantastical imaginations and who share our deep love of reading. This book, and who we became as adults, are all thanks to you.

"This American system of ours, call it Americanism, call it capitalism, call it what you will, gives each and every one of us a great opportunity if we only seize it with both hands and make the most of it."

~ Al Capone

Prologue

"Al Capone murdered me tonight."

I could hear the creak of the chair as the agent leaned forward. His face was in shadow, not that I would have been able to see him anyway. I'm pretty sure that he introduced himself to me, but I forget his name. I couldn't think straight or feel much of anything; drugs, I guessed. I knew that my words were true, but it was just taking my body some time to realize the facts. I could feel the bandage on my head, wrapped too tight, covering my face and wrapping around to cover my left eye. My right eye was swollen to a narrow slit through which I could barely make out my surroundings.

I knew that I was in a hospital; the sharp smell of alcohol and antiseptic assaulted my nose. I was lying in a hospital bed; I could see the white sheets that were stretched over my body and the frame of a white metal bed past my feet. A dim light came from my left, its feeble glow barely reaching the foot of the bed. Something was taped to my left arm, and I could just make out a large bandage across my chest. "*Gevalt!* Mom's going to be pissed at me," I sighed, and then had to laugh at the absurdity of my words.

The man in the shadows spoke. "Mr. Imbierowicz, I need you to tell me exactly how Alphonse Capone murdered you." He didn't seem to be bothered by the incongruity of that statement. Apparently, he could see the same thing that my body had not yet figured out.

"Call me Saul. My father is Mr. Imbierowicz," I said with a croaking rasp. I coughed and pain overcame the drugs and shot through my chest. I had a metallic taste in my mouth and I spat out a glob of blood and phlegm across the white bedding. Somebody to my left held a glass of water with a straw to my mouth. I smelled the scent of lavender and caught a glimpse of red hair. My heart leapt, but it was quickly dashed as an unfamiliar voice said, "Here, drink this."

I sipped the water slowly, letting it quench my parched lips and wash the bloody taste from my mouth. I got too greedy and water dribbled down my chin, which was quickly wiped away by my red-haired imposter. "Not too quickly, you'll have plenty of time to finish." *She's obviously not a doctor, I mean, has she even seen me?*

At that point a blurry figure stepped up to the bed, lifting a clipboard. I could hear pages being flipped. A man's voice said, "There's nothing more we can do for him. At best we can make him comfortable. You need to leave."

"No," the seated man said. "I need Mr. Imbierowicz to tell me what happened." His voice was sharp and authoritative.

"As his doctor I insist that you let him be." The doctor's voice had risen to match my visitor's authoritative tone. *Here I am, literally lying in my death bed, and these two schmucks are getting in a pissing match over how soon I would die. If I was a betting man, I'd take the under on my dying in an hour.*

The shadow in the chair stood and moved away

2

from me, grabbing the doctor by the arm. I could hear muffled voices from across the room. Heated whispers at first, then the doctor clearly saying, "Very well, but it's on your head."

I convulsed in a coughing fit. Pain pounded through the drugs. More blood came up, and again the straw was held to my lips. Before I could take a sip the doctor commanded, "Nurse, see to your other patients." I heard the glass being set on the table, and then watched my red-headed vision walk out of the room. Even partially blind, my good eye lingered on her retreating form. "Too bad I'm already dead," I muttered. I never did get that sip of water.

A few seconds passed and my visitor purposefully cleared his throat. "I'll leave you alone now," said the doctor. "But if anything happens to my patient you need to inform me immediately." I heard footsteps and the door shutting briskly. My visitor returned to his chair and sat down. I watched as he wiped something from his pants, then crossed his legs. "Now that we are alone, Saul, let's start at the beginning." The man's voice was polite, though it had an edge of insistence to it that commanded respect. The chair creaked as he pulled something from a pocket. "I hope you don't mind if I take notes. I want to make sure I get all the details."

I sighed, and stared at the dark ceiling. "What would a *goy* like you want from me? I'm *gornisht*. A nobody." I turned my head toward the table with the lamp.

"I don't think you're a nobody and neither did Al Capone. He has had many men killed over the years, but he only gets personally involved for special cases."

I turned and squinted toward the chair. The man leaned forward, his face still half in shadow. He pulled a pack of Lucky Strikes from his inside jacket and tapped out a cigarette. A match flared, and then he leaned over and placed the lit cigarette in my lips. I took a deep drag, then blew out a stream of smoke. "Normally the condemned man gets his cigarette before being killed, not after." I chuckled, which was a mistake, as pain rippled across my chest. I coughed up more blood, spitting it out around my cigarette.

The chair creaked again as my questioner leaned back. He lit his own cigarette, the flare of his match reflecting in his eyes. "I think there is something special about you Saul. What is it? Why did Al Capone kill you?"

I leaned back into the pillow and closed my eyes, taking another drag on my Lucky. "Until about two weeks ago I was the most unremarkable person in the world. All that changed on February 14." I blew out a stream of smoke. "St. Valentine's Day."

Chapter 1

The cold February air stung my cheeks as I stepped off the L at Sedgwick station. Turning the collar up on my overcoat I moved through the morning commuters waiting to board the L and head to work. I still wasn't used to working the night shift at the Post Office, but at least I didn't have to fight the morning commute.

Sedgwick wasn't my normal stop; I lived a few blocks west and to the south on Racine Avenue, my small apartment overlooking the 'picturesque' North Branch of the Chicago River. Exiting the station, I paused next to the iron pillar supporting the track to get my bearings. I heard the squeal of brakes and the clack of wheels on the tracks as the L left the station.

"Hey, stranger." The voice was silky, with just an edge of seductiveness to it. I turned toward the sound.

"Moira!" I exclaimed. She stood next to the station door, a lit cigarette held lightly in her left hand. Moira wore a cream-colored blouse with a green tie that matched her eyes. She had on riding pants and calf-length brown leather boots. Her red hair was tucked under a green felt cloche hat, with the brim rakishly turned up. Despite the cold weather, she only had on a light brown jacket. "Aren't you cold?" I started to take my coat off to give it to her.

"My valiant knight," she said as she took a drag on

the cigarette and stepped toward me, putting her hand on my chest. I could just make out the subtle scent of her lavender perfume through the harsh cigarette smoke. "But don't bother, Saul. I like the cold weather. It invigorates me." She gave me a playful look with those lovely green eyes, then she grabbed my hand and headed across the street. I struggled to keep up and dodged the fender of a taxi, as well as the driver's curses.

"Try to keep up, Saul," Moira teased. "I'm starved, and there's this great coffee shop up on Clark I want to try."

"We could have had a cup of Joe at the diner at the Post Office, or at Sam's place near my apartment." I know I was whining, but I was cold and tired from working ten hours the night before and didn't like having to come up north to be able to meet Moira. "This place better be good."

Moira gave me a look but didn't say anything. We headed east toward Lake Michigan. At North Clark she turned and headed up the street for about a half a block, finally stopping at a typical coffee shop, the last of the morning regulars heading out for work.

"Yeah, this place looks really special," I quipped.

"Dry up, Saul. This place is really swanky." She smiled, flashing white teeth. "Besides, they have great pie."

We went inside and sat down at a booth. The waitress dragged herself over, obviously put out that she had to deal with more customers. We both ordered coffee. Moira ordered a slice of apple pie, and since I hadn't eaten since my 'lunch' at 2 a.m., I ordered eggs over easy, hash browns, and pancakes.

"My, aren't we hungry," Moira said as the waitress

went to get our coffee.

"I could eat a pig, but I'll settle for eating like one. I don't think my mother would like it if I ate one."

"I don't think this place is Kosher," said Moira, smiling as the waitress set our coffee down with a glare.

I ignored Moira's comment, and added sugar to my coffee. "So, last night when you were leaving my place you said you had something special to tell me. What's up?"

Moira took a sip of her coffee, and then set the cup down. The bell to the shop rang as the last remaining customer left. "Oh, it's nothing important. You are taking me out to dinner tonight, aren't you?"

"I have to work tonight," I protested.

"But its Valentine's Day," she stuck out her lower lip in a pout. "You can take me out to dinner before going to work. I know this place where we can get a real drink."

The waitress returned with my breakfast and Moira's pie. A big piece of ham covered the hash browns and eggs. The waitress gave me a smirk. I frowned, but didn't say anything. She turned away with a laugh.

Moira reached over and grabbed the ham and flung it on the floor. It landed with a dull splat. The waitress started to say something, but Moira stopped her with a look that even gave me chills. The waitress seemed to recoil, then quickly went back to doing something else.

"I'll come to your place at seven and we'll go to the Lexington."

I nearly spit coffee all over Moira at the suggestion. "Who do you think I am, Al Capone? I can't afford to take you there."

Moira laughed and reached across the table to hold my hand. "Honey, you're no Al Capone. But you can take me to the Lexington. I know some people. Don't be such a wet blanket."

"I'm not being a wet blanket," I protested. "You know I just started working at the Post Office. I haven't even gotten my first paycheck yet." I was starting to sound like a wet blanket, but it was the truth. I had been able to pay the rent for my apartment using money that I'd saved from my bar mitzvah, but I needed the paycheck in order to keep it. I was splurging with my breakfast. I usually just grabbed a cup of Joe and a sinker for ten cents from the shop at the Post Office.

Moira just ate her apple pie, looking at me impatiently. *Glaring at me, more like it.* I was starting to feel pretty intimidated by her stare. I picked at my eggs and tried to ignore her, but she continued to watch me. Finally, I couldn't stand it any longer.

"Fine. I'll take you to the Lexington tonight."

Moira smiled and patted my hand, "Of course you will."

"I'm glad to know that I had a choice in this decision."

Moira grinned at me, then raised her coffee cup at the waitress indicating that she wanted a refill. The waitress sheepishly walked over. "I brewed a fresh pot just for you." As she poured the steaming coffee into both of our cups, Moira narrowed her eyes and asked, "Don't you have something to say?" The waitress seemed to pale, lowered her eyes, and said, "I hope you know I was just joshing with you with the ham. I didn't mean anything by it, honest."

"No offense taken. I actually thought it was pretty funny."

"But I didn't," Moira said flatly.

"Can I get you anything else?" the waitress asked nervously.

"Well, the pie was really good," Moira said in a sing-song voice. "So you should bring us two more slices on the house."

"That's not necessary," I protested. "It was just a joke. Nobody was hurt."

"No, that's okay. I'll take care of it," the waitress insisted. She turned and walked toward the counter.

Moira smugly leaned back, shaking her head. "Honestly, Saul. You can't let people push you around like that."

"What? She didn't mean anything by it. She could get in trouble for giving us the pie for free."

Moira just laughed. "Come on, Saul. We deserve it for what she did to you."

I sighed, and decided that it was best to not press the issue any further. I'd be sure to leave enough of a tip to cover the cost of the pie.

The waitress brought two plates with extra-large slices of pie on them. I noticed the white name tag with red letters spelling out "Gladys". "Thank you, Gladys. Can you bring us the check, please?" I asked. She smiled politely and hurried away.

"I think you kind of scared her," I said.

"Good." Moira's fork dug into the pie.

We finished up our breakfast about twenty minutes later. It really hadn't been any better than the shop at the Post Office, and I told Moira that, but she just laughed it off. We spent the time eating our pie and not really talking about anything special. Moira occasionally giggled to herself, and when I asked her what was so funny, she'd just say "Nothing."

Moira and I had met just a week ago and most of our conversations were the same. Small chit-chat and not much else. I guess that was my fault as I spent most of the time just staring at how beautiful she was. Meeting Moira had been part of my lucky week. I started my new job at the Post Office as a mail sorter on the fourth of February. Three days later, I first laid eyes on Moira at the coffee shop at the Post Office. It was love at first sight when she sat down next to me at the counter. And the funny thing was that she thought the same thing.

We saw each other the next couple of mornings at the diner, and I invited her back to my apartment on our third meeting. I was afraid that I was being too forward, but she smiled and said sure. We didn't do anything other than just talk over coffee—though I wanted to do something more. Moira seemed to be more amused than upset by my boyish attempts to kiss her. She laughed it off and said, "In time, tiger."

We went out for dinner and drinks at a speakeasy she knew a couple of nights ago. I had been nervous about going to a speakeasy with her. Not that I was a stranger to drinking or any kind of prude or anything. I was just scared that she'd leave me to sit alone while she went and flirted with better guys. I mean, I'm a pretty good guy, but I'm just an average Joe—plain brown hair, sappy brown eyes, not very tall, and on the skinny side, despite my mom's attempts to fatten me up. Nothing special. I guess I was just still amazed that Moira wanted to be with me. I hadn't needed to worry. Moira had spent the evening chatting and flirting with me. Not that there weren't plenty of opportunities for her to flirt with others. It seemed like every Joe in the joint came up and tried to get her to dance or was trying to buy her drinks. The guys always went away disappointed. The joint—it was called The Green Mill—was not a bad gin mill, and Moira seemed to be great friends with the barman so we got our drinks for free. I knew that night that Moira and I had something special going.

We left the coffee shop and headed back out into the cold. I turned to head back to the L station, but Moira grabbed my arm and headed up the street.

"This way, Saul. There are some friends of mine I want you to meet."

"What? Now?" I asked dumbly. I was wasting a lot of time that would be better spent sleeping, especially if I was taking Moira out tonight.

"Sure. It won't take long."

I shrugged and let her lead the way. I was dead tired, but I couldn't really resist.

"I don't have anything to wear to the Lexington," I mused to Moira. "I've not had a suit since my bar mitzvah, and I don't think I can get into that one anymore."

"Don't worry about it. I'll let you borrow my tie." She shook the green tie she was wearing in my face with an impish smile.

"Ha. Ha," I said. "I'm serious. That place is ritzy, full of rich snobs. Even if I had a suit I wouldn't fit in."

"Don't worry about it," Moira repeated. A black Cadillac passed us heading up the street. Moira turned her back to the road and gave a small shiver.

"Are you sure you're not cold? You can have my coat."

"It's nothing," she said, her voice a bit distant. She pulled out a cigarette and I pulled out my Ronson to light it. She took a long pull on the Chesterfield, blowing the smoke into the frigid air. "Like I said, I know some people at the Lex. They'll make sure we get in and it won't matter what you wear." She leaned over and gave me a slow kiss. My mind swam; it wasn't our first kiss —that had been at the speakeasy—but the other kiss hadn't been like this. I could feel her tongue playfully reaching out and tickling my own tongue.

She broke the kiss and looked past me up the street. I turned but she grabbed my arm and we continued, her right arm entwined in my left. I heard the sound of a car backfiring a couple of times. I glanced up from gazing at Moira and saw the same black Cadillac idling in front of a garage with a sign that read, SMC Cartage Co. Two cops were leading two other men dressed in suits toward the car.

BANG!

I nearly jumped out of my shoes at the sound. One of the men being led by the cops stumbled, a gout of blood shooting from his shoulder. The cops pulled their revolvers and pointed them toward Moira and me. I protectively stepped in front of her as I raised my hands, yelling "Nooo!"

More gunshots exploded around me. The cops fired toward us, and more shots rang out from behind us. Moira's red hair flashed before me and I felt a sharp pain in my chest, falling to the ground. Moira fell on top of me. I cowered, hands over my head as several more shots were fired. I looked up and could see the cops pushing the two men into the car. The men fell in, then one of the cops got behind the wheel, and the other jumped onto the running board and fired two more shots as the car pulled away. I glanced behind me and could see two men running down the street, their overcoats flapping behind them as they ran.

Everything was suddenly quiet except for the frantic barking of a dog coming from someplace nearby. I crawled out from under Moira and gave her a shake. "What the hell was that?" My ears were still ringing from the gunfire. "Come on, let's get out of here."

I shook Moira again. She didn't move. A deep fear settled in my stomach as I turned Moira over. She lay in a pool of blood. A ragged hole was in her left chest, right about where the heart would be. Her blouse was stained red, and her green tie had a sickly, mottled color. "No, no, no," I mumbled. I felt her neck, but I couldn't feel a pulse. "No, no. This didn't happen."

Blood covered my hands and was soaking into the knees of my pants. I could hear the wail of a police siren in the distance. I stood up, muttering "This isn't happening."

The sirens were getting closer. It wasn't safe for me to be here; you never knew what the cops might do, and I didn't want to be there to find out. Panic gripped my heart and I ran across the street and down an alley, fear and dread propelling me away from Moira's dead body.

Chapter 2

I ran for several blocks, my legs carrying me away from the nightmarish scene. I'm sure that I was quite the sight, running through the streets with bloodied clothes, but I didn't care. I saw the diner where Moira had eaten her last meal and I skidded to a stop. Gladys the waitress stood outside the entrance, a cigarette perched on her lips. I started to say something, but the look she gave me, followed by her scream, compelled me to run on. I ran and ran until I couldn't breathe. I finally stopped in an alley, hiding behind a trash bin and away from the people on the street. Bending at the waist, my hands resting on my blood-stained knees, I tried to catch my breath. Images of the gunfight and Moira's blood spreading on the cement played in my head like some demented movie. I gagged on bile, and then vomited behind the bin. I spat out the sick remnants of my breakfast, and then sat down on the cold pavement.

I was dazed and winded, and had a pain in my chest. Suddenly thinking that I might also have been shot, I grabbed at my shirt feeling for a hole or blood. I couldn't help but remember Uncle Jakob telling me about fighting during the Great War and how soldiers would check themselves for wounds after a battle. I pulled up my shirt to look, the cold air biting at my skin, but all I saw was the beginning of a bruise. Moira must have fallen into me when the bullet struck her. I didn't know how she'd gotten in front of me, and I couldn't make sense of why she would have done that.

I don't know how long that I sat there, but eventually I crawled back onto my feet. My first thought was to return to where Moira had been shot. A part of me knew that I should go back and tell the police what had happened, and what I had seen. But if I went back looking like this, the cops would arrest me on sight. Hell, Gladys would probably tell the cops that Moira deserved it after the misery that she put her through this morning, And I'd never get a chance to tell them what really happened. Straightening my clothes, I walked out of the alley as casually as I could and continued home. I didn't remember the rest of the walk, making the necessary turns or crossing any streets to get back to my apartment at 1313 North Racine, but I apparently made it without incident since the next thing I knew I was climbing the stairs to my third floor apartment.

The floor creaked as I reached the second floor landing and I froze. I knew that meant that Mrs. Rabinowitz would know somebody was here and poke her head out. As if on cue, her door cracked open. Mrs. R was a nice old lady who lost her husband last summer, and I think she had been trying to fill the void left by his passing by focusing on my life. *She was worse than my mom in that way.* When I had moved in, she and Mom had met and Mrs. R had promised Mom that she'd look out for me and keep her informed of everything that I did. She was thin and shorter than my sister, with a pronounced stoop to her posture. She had grey hair that was always meticulously pinned up on her head. Normally I would have greeted her warmly and chatted with her about my day, but right now I wasn't in the mood for chit-chat or to listen to one of her lectures. She started to call out to me, but before she could say anything I waved her off, saying, "Not right now, Mrs. R. I'll catch up with you later." I don't know if I stunned her by my abrupt greeting, or if she caught a glimpse of my bloody clothes as I turned to head up the stairs, but she didn't say anything and quickly closed her door.

I unlocked my door, closing it behind me. My apartment was one of two on the top floor of the tenement. It was on the right side of the building, the door from the hall opening onto the small kitchen—sink, small hotplate, an old icebox that actually needed ice to keep anything cold and a few functioning cabinets, which were painted the same odd canary yellow color as the walls.

I had only been in the apartment for about two weeks and hadn't really bothered to decorate. The apartment had come furnished, such as it was, with a table and a couple of chairs in the kitchen, a ratty couch and a floor lamp in the front room of the apartment overlooking the street, and a bed and wardrobe in the bedroom in the back. There were rugs in both the bedroom and the living room, but bare wood floors in the rest of the place. I had brought with me my only possessions: two quilts, one from Nana and the other from Grandma Imbierowicz, my clothes, an alarm clock, and a family portrait of mom and dad standing with me and my younger sister at my bar mitzvah. Mom had reluctantly lent me some dishes, a single coffee cup, one glass, some cutlery, and an old frying pan. She'd have preferred that I ate all of my meals at home, but I had insisted on making my own way.

I pulled the cord for the kitchen light, which cast a feeble glow and gave the yellow walls a sickly hue. I walked over to the sink and picked up the dirty glass that I'd used at breakfast and filled it with water. I raised it unsteadily to my lips and took a quick drink, rinsing the bile from my mouth. I threw my coat over the table and headed for the bathroom. The bath was filled to capacity with a cast iron tub, toilet, and sink. I looked at my face in the cracked mirror; there were small splatters of blood on my cheek. As I turned on the water, I noticed that my hands were caked with dried blood—Moira's blood. I started franticly scrubbing my hands and face, but the blood came off too slowly. I felt dirty all over, covered with blood and drenched in a cold sweat. I tore off my clothes as I ran water in the tub.

The water was cold, but I didn't care. I scrubbed my hands and legs until I had removed all of the blood. The entire time I was re-living the events of the morning. Moira meeting me at the L. The dull slap of a ham steak hitting the diner's tile floor. Moira's glare at the waitress. The cold air and how great it felt when she kissed me. Then the confusion of the gunfight, and the gut-twisting fear when I saw Moira lying in a pool of her own blood.

I almost vomited again, but I had nothing left and just dry heaved a couple of times. I sat in the cold water, catching my breath. "Why did I run away?" I asked the tub.

I didn't expect an answer, but I couldn't help but hear Mom's voice in my head telling me, "Don't be a *shvuntz*. You need to go tell the police what happened. You need to go tell them about this poor girl's death and that you had nothing to do with it."

17

"But the cops were there already," I whined back silently. "They're the ones that shot Moira."

Mom didn't answer. Neither did the tub.

Between the temperature of the water and my slow realization that I would never see Moira again, I was beginning to feel cold. Shivering, I pulled the plug, letting the pinkish water drain out and dried off with a threadbare towel. I left the blood-stained clothes on the bathroom floor and dressed for bed. It was after noon, and I needed to sleep. I wouldn't even have time to mourn Moira's death; I would lose my job if I missed work. I set the alarm clock and crawled under the quilts.

As I drifted off to sleep, a cruel thought came to me. At least I didn't have to go to the Lexington.

Chapter 3

My alarm clock woke me up at 8 p.m. Despite nearly eight hours of sleep I was completely exhausted. I had the strangest dreams, filled with grinning wolves chasing me down endless alleys. As I hurried around a corner I nearly ran into Moira, standing with her hands on her hips and looking at me in the same way that she had looked at the pie that she'd devoured this morning. Needless to say, I hadn't slept well.

I dragged myself out of bed and did my 'morning' routine. I was still getting used to working the graveyard shift. 10 p.m. to 8 a.m. was not a shift that any sane person would like, but it was a job and postal work paid pretty well. At least well enough that I could get out from under Mom and Dad's roof, and it was a far cry better than working at the Armour meat packers like Dad.

I picked up my clothes from the bathroom floor and tossed them into the bottom of the wardrobe. Mom would give me hell about the blood, but I could tell her a lie about how it got on my clothes, and with Dad working forever and a day at the packing house, she knew how to get blood stains out of any piece of clothing. I took a proper bath—one advantage of my shift was that I always had hot water at night—then dressed in clean clothes. I made myself coffee in a rusty, third-hand coffee pot that I'd picked up at a junk shop and pulled a day-old bagel—*well*—*more like three days old*—from the cupboard. I was out the door and heading for another day at the Post Office by 9:30 p.m. I didn't have to worry about Mrs. R stopping me to chat as she was always in bed by 8 o'clock.

I got on the L at the Racine Street station, and took it around the Loop to the Post Office. My mind was still preoccupied with the events of this morning. There was a couple sitting at the back of the train, holding hands. They were dressed for the town, and she held a small bouquet of roses. I suddenly remembered that it was still Valentine's Day and, had events been different this morning, I'd be at the Lexington with Moira right now. The couple caught me staring at them and I awkwardly turned away.

I got off the train and entered the massive Post Office building, taking the stairs up to the third floor where the sorting room was located. The sorting room was a large space filled with dozens of stations where the mail was sorted in order for it to get to its destination. Bags of mail were dumped into wheeled bins that were brought into the sorting room so that the sorters could examine each piece and place it in its proper slot. Once we sorted the mail at night, the mail carriers would pick up the mail in the morning for delivery. I clocked in and headed to my station without talking to anybody. I picked up a stack of letters from the bin and started sorting them into the slots.

"Hey, Saul. Did ya hear the news?"

I looked over to Joe Klein, who stood at the sorting station next to mine. Joe was my co-worker and had become a good friend in the past couple of weeks. He sounded excited.

"What news? You finally get that dame to go out with you?" I laughed. Joe had been trying to get Francine, the waitress from the coffee shop downstairs, to go out with him for forever, or at least for the entire time that I had been here.

"What?" Joe sneered, which was odd since he always liked talking about his soon-to-be girlfriend. "No, the news about the killin'."

My stomach jumped, and I fought back bile in my throat. "What killing," I replied as evenly as I could.

"What killin'?" Joe practically yelled. "How can you not know? What killin'?" Joe sighed and shoved a couple of letters into a slot. "The killin' that's in all the papers. What they're callin' a massacre."

I breathed a bit easier. If Joe was saying it was a massacre, then it couldn't be about Moira's death. "Look, Joe. I had a wonderful date with my beautiful gal after work yesterday, then crashed in bed for the rest of the day until I got up to come here and enjoy your smiling mug. I haven't heard about any massacre, so spill the beans."

Joe leaned over conspiratorially, even though half the sorting room had heard him earlier. "The papers say that seven of Bugs Moran's gang got killed."

I whistled. "Was it another gang?"

"The papers are saying it might be Capone's gang, but there's no proof." Joe grabbed some more letters from the bin. "Hell, I heard that Al has been down in Florida for weeks."

I laughed. Joe always liked to talk like he knew Al Capone personally. "So where'd this massacre take place?" I picked up a new stack of letters.

"Up on North Clark Street in some garage. The Daily

News has got....You okay, Saul?"

I had just dropped the entire stack of letters onto the floor and I felt the blood drain from my face. I quickly knelt down to pick up the letters. *It's just a coincidence,* I told myself. *There's lots of places on North Clark Street where this could have happened.* I stood back up. "I'm fine. I think it's just something I ate."

"That's cuz you Jews don't eat proper food," Joe said, going back to his sorting. "You need to eat some good pork chops or bacon sometime. Maybe a nice slab of ham."

I winced at the memory of Moira flinging the ham to the diner's floor. I went back to sorting and let Joe go on with his rant against my faith. Not that I was especially religious, mind you, since I usually went to Temple just to make Mom happy. I knew that once Joe got started on a new topic he wouldn't come back to talking about the massacre at the garage unless I brought it up.

But now it was hard to concentrate on my work. Did the papers know about Moira too? I kept telling myself that this massacre had to have happened someplace else. I don't know how I managed to get through until our break; my mind was filled with all sorts of dread and fear. I kept glancing toward the sorting room doors, expecting the cops to come busting through to haul me away for questioning.

Joe and I headed down to the coffee shop at lunch. The place was busy as usual. Somebody was getting up from the counter just as we came in and left behind a copy of last night's Daily News. I grabbed the seat before Joe could and looked at the paper. The headline seemed to scream "MASSACRE 7 OF MORAN GANG" and there was a picture of several dead bodies, the wall behind them riddled with bullet holes.

I ordered the special and a cup of Joe. While I waited for my food to come I read through the article. "Killing scene too gruesome for onlookers. View of carnage proves a strain on their nerves. Victims are lined against wall; one volley kills all. Assassins pose as policemen; flee in 'squad car' after fusillade; Capone revenge for murders of Lombardo, officers believe."

The description all fell into place with my jumbled memories from yesterday morning. The sound of the car backfiring must have been gunfire, and the policemen that were leading the two 'criminals' out of the building were probably the assassins. But there was nothing in the article about a shoot out outside of the garage or anything about a dead woman.

The article listed the dead: Peter Gusenberg, Frank Gusenberg, Al Weinshank, John May, James Clark, Arthur Daves, and Frank Porter. But I didn't see the name Moira Kelly. *Where was her name? Did they not include her because she was a dame? How could they have not found the body, or seen the blood?*

My food arrived but I ignored it. *Maybe she's still alive? But there was all that blood and she had no pulse.* A glimmer of hope took root in my mind. The cops were pretty thorough, and the news hounds wouldn't have let a dead woman stop them. Hell, they would have made that the front page headline "WOMAN SLAIN IN GANG WAR", with a graphic picture of the dead woman. *Anything to sell a paper.*

No, Moira had to be alive. *Maybe the cops had gotten her to a hospital?* But now I had a feeling of guilt—not an uncommon thing for the son of a Jewish mother. *If she's not dead, then I left her there, all alone.* I had aban-

23

doned her, and because of me she might have died, or be at death's door even now.

"Hey Saul," Joe grabbed my shoulder.

"Huh?" I looked up from the paper. My dinner was untouched and the coffee was cold.

"Break's over. We gotta go back. You know that Mr. Dickenson will dock you if you're late."

"Yeah, yeah." I stood up.

"You hardly touched your food," Joe said as we headed out of the shop. "You sure you're feelin' okay?"

"Yeah, I'm fine. I just wasn't very hungry." We reached the elevator and I pushed the call button. "I guess that I'm just shocked by all of the crime in our fair city."

Chapter 4

The morning sun filtered through the windows of the sorting room. I finished sorting the last of the letters in my bin, and then turned toward the door.

Joe tossed a stack of letters back into his bin. "Come on Saul, let's go see if my girl can get us some breakfast. I'll even make sure she leaves the pig off your plate."

I winced again at the memory of yesterday's breakfast and hesitated. Our usual morning ritual was to head to the coffee shop. I'd order coffee and a donut, and Joe would spend his time trying to convince his 'girlfriend' to go out with him. She'd lead him on, finding some excuse to say no at the end. I was starting to think that Joe preferred being led on. I don't know what he'd do if she actually said yes. "Um, not this morning Joe." I put my hand on my stomach. "I'm still not feeling well. I'm just gonna go home."

Joe gave me a quizzical look, but smiled and said, "Okay, pal."

He seemed let down, probably because this was the second day in a row I was going to ditch him. "Let me know if your girl says yes this morning."

Joe perked up once I got him thinking about something else. He gave me a wave as I headed out the door.

I was tired and famished. It was after noon and I had

lost track of how many hospitals I had entered. I never knew that there were so many hospitals in Chicago. I'd tried all of the ones in the north—those closest to North Clark Street. I'd gone south to Mercy and St. Luke's. I probably should have gone to Cook County first, but what can I say, I'm not really good at planning stuff out.

I walked into Cook County, the sharp smell of alcohol and antiseptic filling the air. *If I had to smell that all the time I would never want to be in a hospital.* I walked up to a large desk where a bespectacled woman sat. She wore a starched white nurse's uniform and had light brown hair pulled back in a ponytail.

"Hello," I said with a smile. "I'm looking for a woman who might have been admitted here yesterday."

The woman gave me a bored expression as she peered at me over the frame of her glasses, but said, "Name?"

"Moira Kelly. She might have come in at the same time as that gang killing up on Clark Street."

She looked at a ledger book, her finger tracing down a list of names. "Nobody here by that name." She set the book aside.

"She has red hair," I persisted. "And she would have had a gunshot wound."

The woman gave me a shocked look. An orderly wheeled a gurney past the desk. "I'm sorry, sir," she said. "But the only person who came in yesterday with a gunshot wound was that man there." She pointed to the gurney as it passed the desk, and leaned closer to me, whispering, "Only he had fourteen bullet holes in him." She sat back down, "and he died yesterday afternoon." She went back to her work.

I almost collapsed from exhaustion. Hope had been

the only thing keeping me going, and she'd just burst that bubble. I mumbled, "Thanks anyway," which she ignored, and I staggered outside.

The air was sharp and cold, but it did little to relieve my weariness. Instead, I felt numb all over. I couldn't come to terms with the two contradictory thoughts in my head; that Moira had to be alive because there had been no body found at the scene, and that she had to be dead because she wasn't in any of the hospitals.

I headed up the street, wandering aimlessly but subconsciously in the general direction of my apartment. All the while a commentary ran through my head. *Maybe somebody in the neighborhood saw her and took her in to treat her?* "And what, these kind strangers were doctors and surgeons?" My mother's voice mocked me.

I should go to the police to see if maybe they had found the body and had somehow convinced the press to keep it out of the papers. "Don't be a *schmendrek*," my father's voice taunted me. "You want them to question you about what happened and why you ran away? That's not what somebody who is not guilty of something does."

I waved the thought away as if swatting at an annoying gnat, pulling off my cap and scratching my head in thought. *I don't know what to do. Should I check the morgue?* My Dad's voice persisted, "You'd face the same questions there as if you'd gone to the police, though they can't arrest you there." *The only other place for me to check is Moira's place.* "But honey, you don't even know where that poor girl lived," Mom chided me. *Lived? What do you mean lived? Moira's still alive!* "Okay, honey. If you say so."

I shook my head, finally clearing my parent's voices from it. *A guy can't catch a break.* I moved out so I could get away from my mother's patronizing tone, but apparently I managed to bring it with me. I continued to wander, eventually reaching my apartment. My legs felt like rubber, and all I could think about was how wonderful my bed would feel as I fell into it. I begrudgingly forced my legs to drag me up the three flights of stairs. I paused on the landing of the third floor, realizing that Mrs. R hadn't come out to greet me. I didn't worry about it, as I was grateful that she wouldn't delay me from reaching my bedroom. My neighbor seemed to be taunting me; I could smell coffee brewing in the hall. As I put my key in the door, it pushed open. I hadn't turned the key to unlock it.

I stepped into the kitchen, a little slowly due to fatigue. The kitchen light was on, the bare bulb casting its harsh light on the canary yellow cupboards and walls. Two strange men were sitting in my only kitchen chairs, their hats perched on my kitchen table. They each had coffee in front of them, and since I only had one coffee cup, one was using my only glass. The one on my right, who had the glass, was a broad-shouldered man wearing an ill-fitting brown suit, with a white shirt and ugly red tie. He looked like some of the guys my dad worked with who carried entire sides of beef from the cutting floor to the freezer. He had a distinctive face; he had broken his nose so many times that it seemed to point to his right ear.

The one on my left, holding my coffee cup, was a bit smaller, but still as formidable. His suit was better cut, a dark blue color with a matching tie. His brown eyes seemed to pierce through me over the brim of the cup. Glass looked tough, but Cup's intensity scared me more.

Cup set his coffee down and said, "Your coffee tastes

like shit, Mr. Imbierowicz."

I know I was tired because I said, "Well, I didn't ask you to drink it, *momzer*."

Glass must have known some Yiddish because he nearly jumped out of his chair, his fists clenched and ready to knock my block off. Luckily for me, Cup either didn't know that I'd just called him a bastard, or he didn't care. He held up his hand and Glass relaxed, though he didn't sit back down.

Cup picked up his coffee and drained it, setting it back down with a grimace on his face. He stood up, grabbing his fedora and placing it on his head. "You need to come with us, Mr. Imbierowicz."

Fatigue must have given me a backbone. "I know you two aren't cops, so in this town that makes you hoods. I've had a long day, I'm tired, and I just want to go to bed. So fuck off."

Glass glared at me, but Cup just snickered. "You are either brave or stupid," he looked at me closely. "Or maybe a little bit of both." I could see the butt of a gun protruding from a holster under his left arm as he pulled on his overcoat.

"Let's go," Cup said to Glass, who stepped toward me, forcing me into the hall. Cup reached up and clicked off the light, then stepped out behind us, pulling the door shut and locking it. He pulled my key out of the lock and handed it to me. "We don't want to keep Mr. Moran waiting."

Chapter 5

Glass led the way down the stairs. Cup gestured with his hand for me to go in front of him. To any onlooker it would have looked like Cup was being polite and letting me go first. He hadn't moved his hand toward his gun, or raised his voice, or done anything to make me think that he'd hurt me. Somehow, I knew that he wouldn't hesitate one second to do any of that if I tried to be difficult.

I was too tired to be difficult. I headed down the stairs after Glass, with Cup a few steps behind me. At this point I really didn't care. I wasn't a fan of pain and had no intention of testing my limits with these two. When we passed the second floor landing, I saw a shadow move under Mrs. R's door. I realized now that my surprise visitors were the reason that she hadn't come out to greet me on my way home.

As we descended the stairs I said, "So why does Mr. Moran want to see me?" Now that the shock of finding two men in my apartment and drinking my coffee had worn off, I had become curious as to why the notorious "Bugs" Moran wanted to see a nobody like me.

Cup said, "It's none of your business why. You just need to come when summoned, like a good dog." He actually patted me on my head as he said the last part. I tried to slap the hand away, and Cup just laughed.

I interpreted Cup's words to mean that he really didn't know why Moran wanted to see me. He was nothing more than an errand boy. A nicely dressed and well-armed errand boy to be sure, but still an errand boy.

Like everyone else in Chicago, I had a good idea of who George "Bugs" Moran was; the papers had made sure of that. He was the ruthless, some said crazy—thus the moniker "Bugs"—leader of the North Side Gang, and perpetual enemy of Al Capone.

Moran had been the sole leader of the North Siders ever since Vincent Drucci had been killed by a cop almost two years before. He was said to have a bad temper, and the papers said that he was responsible for the shootings and deaths of several known Capone henchmen. Of course, the cops didn't have anything on him, but everybody in Chicago knew that Moran was the second most dangerous man in the city, after Al Capone of course.

We reached the bottom of the stairs and headed outside. Glass turned and walked to a light blue and maroon Packard 343 convertible with its top up. "Nice car," I commented. Glass didn't say anything, but opened the back door and gestured with his meaty hand for me to get in. I obliged, noting the nice leather interior. "I guess crime really does pay."

"Everybody's a comedian," Cup said as he got in next to me. Glass went around and got behind the wheel. The Packard started with a low rumble and Glass pulled away from the curb.

Glass turned the car east on West Chicago Avenue driving steadily through the mid-afternoon traffic. We crossed the river, and at North Lasalle, he turned left. "Where are you taking me?" I asked. I didn't expect a response, or at most a snide remark from Cup, but I was tired of the silence.

"We're going to Mr. Moran's place at The Parkway."

Wow, an actual answer. I didn't know if that was a good sign or a bad sign.

We crossed North Avenue, and then drove along Lincoln Park on North Clark. A chill ran up my spine thinking back to the events of yesterday morning. I distracted myself by looking towards the park. Despite the cold a few intrepid people were out walking, trying to enjoy the weak February sun.

Glass turned the car onto Lincoln Park West and we pulled up in front of The Parkway. Glass turned off the ignition and got out, opening the rear door. Cup gave me a slight nudge, and I exited the car. The three of us walked through the hotel entrance, Glass a little ahead to call for the elevator.

Once it arrived, we got into the elevator and rode it all the way to the top floor. Glass stayed put when the door opened, but Cup headed down the hall. I dutifully followed. I really didn't have a choice; I had no escape route even if I thought there was a chance that I could get away. Honestly, by this point I was really curious as to why the city's second biggest gangster wanted to see me.

Cup stopped in front of an ornately decorated door and knocked. Not waiting for a response, he opened it and gestured for me to enter. I walked into a small entry room that was populated with a few straight-backed chairs, a side table holding a vase of white lilies and red tulips, and a brass coat rack. Cup walked in behind me and hung his coat on the rack. Closing the door, he said. "Mr. Moran is waiting for you in the study." He pointed down the hall.

I gave Cup a look and asked, "What, you're not coming with me?"

He only shrugged and said, "He didn't ask for me." He picked up a copy of the Tribune from one of the chairs and sat down in it. I caught a glance of the headline "SLAY DOCTOR IN MASSACRE". I hesitantly walked down the hallway. My stomach felt like it had a swarm of butterflies in it as I entered the study.

The room was dimly lit by a chandelier hanging from the ceiling. A large desk sat to the left, and a leather sofa was on the right. The room was thickly carpeted and a fur-trimmed coat hung from a coat stand next to me. Across the room from me, a man with a cigar in his hand stood in front a window.

"Mr. Imbierowicz," the man said as he turned around, his features in shadow. "Why does the Beast want you alive?"

Chapter 6

Moran walked over to the desk and sat down. As he stepped into the light I could now see him clearly. His face was round, the cheeks a bit pudgy. He wore a white shirt and a dark blue vest. A spotted tie was loosely knotted around his neck, which failed to cover a scar on the right side. *And they call Capone "Scarface"*.

"Please, sit down, Mr. Imbierowicz. Would you like a cigar?" Moran indicated the lit cigar in his hand as I sat down on the couch.

"No, thank you." I was taken aback by his pleasant demeanor.

"Mrs. Imbierowicz taught you well, I see. That's good. I like a man who knows his place." He gave me a hard look, like a man would give to a dog to make sure that it knew its master. *At least he didn't pat me on the head.*

"Yes, sir." It wasn't the height of witty banter, I know, but I was doing my best just to keep from pissing my pants.

"Al Capone is an animal. Everybody in Chicago knows he's behind that massacre yesterday, even though he's in Florida. Nobody but me has the balls to do anything about it." He took a drag on his cigar and set it in the ashtray on his desk. "Capone has no moral scruples. I might get a bit angry from time to time, and I'm not afraid of a little violence," he touched the scar on his neck. "But I'd never pull a stunt like the one that he pulled yesterday."

I bit my tongue as I recalled Moran's hundred car procession a few years ago that had shot up Capone's hotel in Cicero. I thought about it, but I wisely didn't mention it. *I guess my mom did teach me well.* Instead, I said, "And how does this pertain to me, Mr. Moran?"

"Ah, right to the point I see." He chuckled. I was getting a little annoyed by the number of people laughing at me today.

"A few weeks ago, the Chicago cops got smart and conducted a raid up north on some of Capone's slot-machine interests."

I nodded, like I knew what the hell Moran was talking about.

"During the raid, the cops managed to snag some of the books that little Ralphie Capone had carelessly left there. In another miracle of cooperation and intelligence, the cops gave the books to the Feds. The Feds now have a thread that they can use against Ralphie to start tugging at Capone's organization." Moran stood up and grabbed the cigar from the ashtray. He walked around his desk and leaned against it, pointing at me with the tip of his cigar.

"That's where you come in, Mr. Imbierowicz."

"I'm sorry sir, but I still don't understand. I work at the Post Office as a mail sorter. Other than what I read in the paper, I don't know anything about Capone's gang or the Feds."

"Ah, but you managed to stand between Capone's goons and my people yesterday morning and came away without a scratch."

"That was pure luck," I blurted out. "My girlfriend

and I were walking down the street and just stumbled into that gunfight."

"And your girlfriend saved your life," Moran remarked. "She saved it for Capone."

"What?" I stood up from the couch, shocked, and a bit upset at what Moran was saying. "Moira doesn't work for Capone! She probably knows less about Capone and gangs in Chicago than I do."

Moran chuckled again. "What's so damn funny?" I yelled. I was getting tired of all this bullshit.

"The Feds have taken their little care package to an office in the Post Office building. Capone was looking for somebody—you precisely—to get that package for him so that the Feds wouldn't be able to build their case against Ralphie."

"I just started barely a week ago. Capone can't have been looking to use me," I protested.

"You should look into what happened to the man you replaced." I started to say something, but Moran waved his cigar to silence me. "I want to make sure that Ralph Capone goes down. To do that, I need you to steal these books for me. I'll make sure that they get to a lawyer who I can trust to keep them out of Capone's mitts."

I sat back down on the couch, stunned. "Wait. Capone was going to get *me* to steal these books for *him*, and now *you* want me to do the same thing?" *What was I getting dragged into?*

"Exactly." Moran walked over to the window. "Capone was using your girlfriend to get information about you. Knowing Capone's style, he was probably going to kill your dad and threaten your mom in order to get you to do what he wanted."

"This can't be happening," I put my head in my hands.

"Thankfully for you it won't happen like that, as long as you do as I say." Moran turned to look at me. "All I'm gonna do is tell you that if you don't do as I ask, your parents will be killed. See how more civilized that is? No bloodshed is needed and we'll both get what we want."

I raised my head to see Moran smiling at me. He put his cigar into his mouth and took a long pull. *This is not happening to me.* My head was spinning and I felt like I was going to throw up.

Yesterday morning my life was great; I had a new job and a beautiful girlfriend. Then I end up in the middle of a gunfight, my girlfriend dies, and I find out that not just one, but two of the biggest gangsters in Chicago are both after me to steal the same thing for them from the Feds. *What the hell is happening to me?*

"Please use that smart head of yours your mamma gave you," Moran said. "I want those books, and if I don't get them I will make sure that the next time that you see your parents will be at their funeral."

"I'll do it," I squeaked out. *Like I have a choice.* I stood up unsteadily. "But I need a couple of days to find out where in the building the Feds are holed up and see how to get my hands on the books."

"Just make sure you let me know if Capone comes sniffing around."

I turned to go. "And Mr. Imbierowicz," Moran called after me. I stopped and looked back at him.

"Next time, you should take better care of your girl-friend."

37

Chapter 7

Cup met me in the entry room, neatly folding up his paper and setting it on the table, then opening the door out into the hall. We met Glass by the elevator doors and we retraced our journey down to the lobby and out to the car. I opened the back door and got in without being told or asked. Glass just laughed under his breath and Cup shrugged as they got in and started the car. Glass pulled the Packard away from the curb and we headed back down south.

My mind was still spinning. So many things had happened to me in the past 36 hours, I didn't know where to start. Suddenly my life was not my own to lead and that pissed me off; but I didn't know what I could do about it.

Going to the cops was such a laughable thought that I didn't even consider it. First, I was sure it would be nearly impossible to find a cop that wasn't getting some graft from either Capone or Moran, so as soon as I told them my story their bosses would know and I'd be in even more hot water. And even if I was lucky enough to find the one clean cop in all of Chicago, what could I say to make them take me seriously? "You could try the truth," my Mom's voice practically yelled in my head. *Like that would work.* Even if they did believe my story, and it was hard to think that they would—I had lived it and I was finding it hard to believe—what kind of protection could the cops give me and my family from the likes of Moran and Capone?

Now that Moran had made his offer to me I could always go to Capone instead; but how could I protect my family if I just gave Capone what he wanted? Why should he care what happened to a couple of Jews? If I give the books to Capone, Moran would keep his promise to kill my parents and Capone would have no reason to protect them. If I give the books to Moran, I face the same dilemma as Capone would just kill my parents and Moran wouldn't bother to protect them.

Glass turned onto West Chicago, heading toward the river. I thought about going to the Feds, but that seemed just as bad as going to the cops. *What would I say?* "Bugs Moran and Al Capone both want me to steal some books you guys have that used to belong to Ralph Capone and they've both threatened to kill my parents if I don't do it." Even if they took me at my word, and that would be a long shot, they couldn't protect my parents any better than the cops could.

I could always try to convince my parents to head up to Milwaukee to stay with Uncle Jakob. "And I should miss work to do this?" I could hear my father complain. "Besides, it's even colder up there. Why your Uncle wants to live in that frozen wasteland is beyond me." *Yeah, I don't see that happening.*

Cup nudged me and pointed to the open car door. It took me a moment to realize that we had stopped moving. I pulled myself across the leather seat and climbed out of the Packard, heading for the door to my tenement.

"Hey Saul," Cup's voice called. I turned around. "I hope it's alright if I use your Christian name, now that you're working for Mr. Moran." He paused. "Though I suppose you don't actually have a Christian name, do ya?" He laughed and I just stood there, numb with fatigue and cold.

Cup pulled out a matchbook and tossed it at me. It hit me in my chest and fell to the ground. I bent over and picked it up. The matches had the name of a dry cleaners over on Dearborn Avenue. "When you get done with your job for Mr. Moran, call us there. We'll come pick you up." He got in the front of the Packard and Glass pulled away.

The sun was setting and I'd been awake for nearly 24 hours. I put the matchbook in my pocket and headed up the steps to my apartment. As I stopped on the landing to pull my key from my pocket, I froze; I could see light coming from under my door. My mind raced as I tried to remember if Cup had turned off the light when we left earlier, but to no avail.

At this point, I was too damn tired to care. I unlocked the door and practically jumped out of my skin at the sight of Mrs. Rabinowitz sitting at my kitchen table reading the evening edition of the Tribune. "Geez, Mrs. R., you scared the life out of me." I grabbed my chest, wondering if my heart would stop racing. "What are you doing in my place?"

"Saul, this is how you treat your neighbors? Leave them sitting here for hours on end waiting for you show up?"

"Mrs. R.," I said in exasperation, "I didn't invite you over. And how the... how did you get in?" I had almost said "how the hell" but I remembered my manners. Mom would be so proud.

She either was ignoring my question or didn't hear

me. "Your mother came by earlier to see you, but you weren't here. I let her in to wait, telling her I'd that seen you go out with a couple of friends. You know, those two well-dressed young men you were with earlier."

I sighed and sat down. "Why are you here?" I asked as slowly as I my dwindling patience would allow.

"You should put another lock on your door, Saul, like I did. A two-year-old could unlock your door. I put my second lock on last summer when Mr. Wolenski came home a bit too drunk and passed out in my living room instead of his." She folded her hands, the silver bracelet that Mr. Rabinowitz had given her for some anniversary or another clicking on the tabletop. "I had Mr. Hooper from the hardware store come and install it..."

"Mrs. Rabinowitz," I interrupted her, almost yelling. I was starting to forget my manners.

"Yes, dear?" She looked at me with soft grey eyes.

"Why. Are. You. In. My. Apartment?" I stressed each word, punctuating the question so she should would understand.

"Oh that," she waved a hand at me. "Like I said, your mother came by to see you, but when you hadn't returned by 4 o'clock she said that she had to leave so that she could get home in time to make dinner for your father and sister. So she asked me to leave you a message."

I put my left hand to my face, running it from my cheek to under my hat. "Why didn't you just write the message down for me?"

She looked at me like I was an idiot. "And how exactly would you expect me to do that, dear? You don't have any paper and there's not a pencil to be found in this place. So I went downstairs and got my newspaper and came back to wait for you."

41

I pulled my hat off and sighed again. I desperately needed to get some sleep before work, and that would only happen once Mrs. R. left. "And what was the message?" I asked as slowly, and as politely, as I could.

"She asked me to remind you that you are to stop by Mr. Sandusky's to pick up the challah for lunch tomorrow. And you need to make sure you make it to Temple this week." She pointed a crooked finger at me, almost the perfect imitation of how Mom did it.

"Thank you for telling me, Mrs. R.," I said. I needed her to leave so that I could go to sleep. I'd worry about not making my Mom madder at me later.

"You're welcome, dear." She stood up and grabbed her paper then opened the door. "You really should go by Mr. Hooper's store and get another lock for this door. It's not safe."

"I'll do that," I lied. "Right after I get the challah tomorrow." I lied again. I hadn't been to Temple for nearly a month and I really had no plans to go tomorrow. Besides, I needed to find a way to get those books from the Feds to make sure that Mom and Dad would be able to continue going to Temple for the foreseeable future.

"Good night, Saul," Mrs. Rabinowitz said as she walked out and headed down the stairs.

"Good day, Mrs. R." I shut the door behind her and locked it. I turned off the light in the kitchen and made my way into the bedroom. I barely managed to set my alarm clock for 9:30 p.m. before I crashed onto the bed with my clothes still on. I was asleep almost instantly.

Chapter 8

I awoke with a start to an insistent clanging sound. It took me a moment to realize that it was my alarm clock going off. I turned it off and lay back on the bed until I suddenly remembered that I had to get to work. The fear of losing my job surged through me and I jumped up and headed to the kitchen. I grabbed my coat, remembered to lock the door on the way out, and ran down the stairs.

I ran down Racine and managed to just make the L, leaping on just as the doors were closing. An older lady gave me a dirty look; I shrugged and gave her an apologetic smile. I sat down and managed to catch my breath by the time the L reached the Post Office. I joined the rest of the shift as we entered the building and clocked in.

I walked over to my sorting station. Joe was already there, sorting a pile of envelopes. "Man, what happened to you?"

I paused, looking at him. "What do you mean?"

"You look like you just downed some coffin varnish."

I shrugged. I couldn't deny that I looked like I had gotten hold of some bad whiskey. I had seen my reflection on the L: puffy eyes from lack of sleep, messed up clothes, and hair like I'd just slept in a gutter. I tried to stifle a yawn and failed, so instead I picked up some letters and started to sort them. "I didn't get a lot of sleep and I almost overslept." Which was enough of the truth that I didn't feel compelled to fill in any of the details. I figured that the less that Joe knew, the better. I didn't want to risk getting him involved in this whole mess.

"You liar," Joe chided me. He tossed a couple of letters carelessly into a box.

"I'm not lying," I said, a little too defensively, so that the only way it could sound was that I was lying to him.

"Come on, man. You can tell me." He winked at me. "You spent your day getting it on with that gal of yours. What's her name?"

"Moira." I relaxed. I was afraid that somehow Joe had known about my encounter with Bugs Moran. It was funny, I thought, that I felt more comfortable telling a lie about my dead girlfriend than I did in telling the truth. "Yeah, I was with her" I said.

"Well," Joe prodded me as he picked up a new stack of letters. "Don't keep the details to yourself." I was going to have to give Joe more than that in order to keep him from digging any further.

I managed to spin a good enough lie to both satisfy Joe and make me long to hold Moira again. It wasn't difficult to tell a convincing story about Moira. Even though we only had our first 'real' kiss just yesterday, I had fantasized enough about her in the past week to fill in the blanks. I told Joe a great line about Moira and I making out at a speakeasy.

"And what about you?" I deflected. "Did your girl-friend say yes this morning?"

"Naw," Joe grabbed a pile of letters and carelessly tossed them into another bin, his thoughts focused on Francine. "She said she had to go home and weed her window box. She's quite the horta....hurtacul....flower person."

I laughed to myself. Poor Joe. He was so in love with that doll that he couldn't see that she wanted nothing to do with him. *Weed her window box? In February?* Apparently she was running out of good excuses too. "Maybe you should find out what her favorite flower is and bring it for her one night," I suggested before I realized what I had done. *Great, now he's gonna be bugging me for the rest of the night to help him find out what her favorite flower is.*

By the time our lunch break came, I was pissed off at myself. I had created a monster. Joe had spent the last several hours speculating on what Francine's favorite flower might be, and how he'd find out, and how she'd finally agree to go out with him once he delivered a dozen of those flowers to her. At least his continuous monologue kept me awake.

I headed down with Joe to the coffee shop. We grabbed two seats at the counter and ordered coffee. I lit up a cigarette and took a long drag. The tobacco gave me a jolt and cleared my head. I blew out a thin cloud of smoke. *Man, these things are great for staying awake. I wonder why we can't smoke while we work?*

"Should I ask George if he knows what kind of flowers she likes?" Joe asked. George was the short order cook who worked the night shift.

"Sure. He might have the inside scoop," I said. I wanted to spend my break seeing if I could find the Feds office and I couldn't do that with Joe tagging along—and he'd insist on it. But if I could get him to pester George with a ton of questions, maybe I could get away.

George set our coffees down. I pointed to a slice of rhubarb pie which he obligingly set down as well. I dropped twenty cents on the counter which George scooped up.

"Hey, George," Joe started. "You know Francine, right?"

George looked at Joe as if he had a screw loose. "Are you nuts? 'Course I know Francine, seeing as she works here every morning."

Joe reddened a bit but trudged on. "So, you know what sorts of things she likes, you know, like her favorite color or drink. Or what her favorite flower is?"

I chuckled as I finished off my pie. I was so hungry that I'd practically inhaled the whole thing. I tuned their conversation out. I knew that George enjoyed seeing Joe squirm under Francine's persistent refusal to go out with him as much as I did, and I knew that Joe was as stubborn as a bulldog once he got an idea in his skull. I downed my coffee and stubbed out my cigarette.

I slid off the stool as Joe turned away to continue his discussion with George as he tried to handle the 'lunch' crowd. Unseen by either of them, I headed out the door and back into the Post Office. I had about twenty minutes before I needed to get back to my shift.

I was pondering how I should go about searching for where the Feds were located when I walked by the information booth in the main hall. The hall was a large, grand space decked out all in grey and white marble. It was a hive of activity during the day, but it was as quiet as a tomb right now. At one end of the hall were the doors that led to the main post office. At the other end was a wide set of stairs leading up to different offices. In the center was a circular booth made of wood and brass, with INFORMATION written in black letters on a frosted glass pane. I had passed through this hall many times; either as a customer getting mail, or when I had come for my job interview. I had never really paid any attention to the information booth before, but now an idea struck me.

I lifted the counter and stepped into the booth. During the day, it was staffed by a guy who was an army veteran and had lost his left arm in the war. He seemed like a nice guy, though I didn't know his name. I searched around his desk, lifting up some papers and looking under a ledger book. I was about to give up when I saw a small, hand-printed note card pinned to a cork board just under the counter. 'Revenue Agents – Room 613 '

I couldn't believe my luck. I left the information booth and headed to the elevators. The sorting room was on the third floor, but when the elevator arrived I punched the button for the sixth. *Maybe I'll get lucky again and I'll be able to grab the books tonight, give them to Moran's goons in the morning, and be done with all of this business in time to piss off Mom by missing Temple.*

The doors opened onto the sixth floor. The hallway was in deep shadow, only lit by a couple of lights. I looked at the numbers painted on the walls and turned to the right. *605, 607, 609...* I turned the corner and saw two doors, one on the left and one at the end of the hall. The door on the left was marked 611 and was stenciled with 'Office of Postal Inspector'. The door at the end of the hall was simply marked 'Janitor' with no number. "What the hell?" I mumbled. I tried the Janitor's door, but it was locked. I then tried the Postal Inspector's door, but it was also locked.

Disappointed, I headed back to the elevators, checking all the door numbers as I went. I then headed down to the left checking those numbers as well. Lots of doors, some with department names and others with names of individuals, but none marked with 613. "Maybe that vet got the number wrong?" I said to myself.

Suddenly, I heard the elevator door open with a clang. I froze, although I don't know why. Technically I was in a public place, but somehow I knew that I would be in trouble if I was seen. I heard a pair of voices, though I couldn't catch what they were saying. They sounded like they were heading toward the Postal Inspector's Office.

As quietly as I could, I headed down the hall and peered around the corner. I saw a man's leg disappear around the corner at the far end of the hall. I headed toward them, passing the elevator, trying to move as quietly as I could on the linoleum floor. I stopped at the corner, listening.

"You ask me, we're going about this in the wrong way." The voice was gruff and raspy, as though the speaker was either a really heavy smoker or somebody from the war who'd been in a gas attack.

"But the Director told us to look into this personally." The second voice was higher in pitch and sounded younger.

"Yeah, yeah." I heard the sound of a key in a lock. I wanted to see who was talking, but I didn't dare look around the corner in case they saw me. "Listen kid, when you've been around the block as long as I have you'll know to trust your gut in these cases, and right now my gut-" Gruff's voice was cut off as the door closed.

I risked a glance around the corner. At first I didn't see anything. "Damn," I swore under my breath. Then

I noticed a thin sliver of light coming from under the door labeled 'Janitor'.

"You sneaky sons of bitches," I smiled. I thought about going up to the door and trying to listen to what they were saying, but I figured that I'd spent enough time searching. My break had to be almost over by now. If I got fired, I wouldn't be able to help either Moran or Capone, and I was sure that neither of them would be sympathetic to my plight.

I headed back to the elevator. As I pushed the call button, I tensed. *Was that the sound of the janitor's door opening?* "Come on, come on," I mumbled to the elevator under my breath. I was sure that the elevator was being slow on purpose.

The elevator finally arrived. I dashed in just as the doors opened, and began repeatedly pushing the button for the third floor.

"So then the dame said, 'over his dead body'." I heard Gruff's laugh. *Oh come on, hurry up you damn mechanical lift!.* I pushed the 3 button harder and the doors started closing. *Hey—it must have done some good.*

"Oh, come on, man," Gruff's voice was getting louder. "That was a funny joke."

They were getting closer. Thankfully, the doors finally closed and the elevator began to descend. I leaned against the elevator's wall, my heart racing. I definitely was not cut out to be a thief or a spy or anything like that.

The doors opened on the third floor, and I stepped out right in front of Joe, who was coming up the steps.

"Where'd you run off to?" Joe asked.

"Uh, nowhere. Just the bathroom."

"Don't bullshit me," Joe said. "I was just in there and

you wasn't."

"Yeah, sure, 'cuz I was in there earlier. Then I went outside for a smoke," I tried to recover, and hoped to redirect Joe's attention. "So did you find out from George what Francine's favorite flower is?"

"Uh, uh." Joe wagged his finger. "Where'd you go? You've been acting strange ever since your date on Valentine's Day. What happened on that date?"

I stalled as we walked into the sorting room. I knew that Joe was not going to let me off easy, or let me change the subject. I was going to have to give him something good to keep him happy. I couldn't tell him the truth, although I was sure that Joe would believe me. There was no way in hell that was I going to drag him down with me.

I stepped up to my sorting station. "Man, I'm sorry if I've been a sap the past few days. You know how it is when you're head over heels about a dame."

Joe chuckled at his station as he sorted through a pile of large envelopes. "Don't you know it!"

"So, Moira and I met for coffee Thursday morning. She said that she had something important to tell me, but she wouldn't tell me what it was at breakfast. You know how women can be." I heard an affirmative grunt from Joe.

"She said that I had to wait until dinner, and you'll never guess in a million years where she wanted me to take her. Come on, guess."

"I don't know, Jake's Diner over on Wacker?" Joe laughed.

"Come on, don't be a goof. She wanted me to take her to The Lex." I heard a gasp from Joe, followed by the sound of several envelopes hitting the floor.

"No way! What did you tell her?" Joe was kneeling down and picking up the fallen envelopes.

"I told her hell no," I laughed. "I haven't even gotten my first paycheck yet. There's no way I could afford to take her there." Up to this point I'd been pretty truthful with Joe, but that had to change. "She gave me some sappy, puppy dog eyes, and pouted like a champ, but I wouldn't give in."

"That's right, man," Joe agreed. "You have to make sure the dames know their place."

I nodded, though I personally didn't agree with Joe. "Instead, I told her I'd take her to this little Italian place I know over on LaSalle. A nice, quiet mom and pop place. So that's what I did. Great food, candles on the table, and even a guy who plays the violin."

"Yeah, I know that place. Called Corleone's, right? Maybe I should take Francine there on our first date."

"So anyway, during the meal Moira tells me that she has to leave town for a while." Since she had been shot and killed, I figured that having her leave town worked in my favor. "I was shocked, 'cuz we'd been hitting it off really well. She told me that she had to go down to Springfield to stay with her sick aunt for a while. But you know how dames are. I couldn't tell if she was telling me the truth or just trying to dump me."

"Man, if Francine tried that on me I don't know how I'd react."

I laughed to myself. Joe was talking like he and Francine were already an item. I figured now was as a good time as any to turn the spotlight back on him. "So, did George tell you anything about what Francine likes?"

Joe began a long discourse on all that he knew about what Francine did and didn't like. I focused on my sorting, letting him drone on. I was happy to not have to talk about Moira any more. Her death still didn't seem real to me, and with all the other stuff that had happened, I was still coming to grips with the whole affair.

Now that I knew where the Feds were hiding out in the building, I just had to figure out how to break into their room, find the books, steal them, and get them to Moran before he decided to make his threat against my parents real. *Piece of cake.*

Chapter 9

I stifled a yawn as Joe and I walked out of the sorting room. I was so tired that I had nearly fallen asleep several times standing at my post. Only the fear of falling down and making a fool of myself, and quite possibly getting fired, kept me going. I desperately wanted to go home and sleep, but I knew that if I ditched Joe again this morning he'd never forgive me. We walked into the diner, which was doing a brisk morning business, and we managed to grab a booth that was being vacated by three mailmen getting ready to start their shift. I slid their empty plates and drained cups of coffee to the side of the table, but Joe's eyes were immediately drawn to Francine, who was walking up with a coffee pot.

Francine is a good lookin' gal, I guess. She didn't have anything on Moira, in my opinion, but I could see why Joe was interested. She had soft brown hair that she wore pulled together into a ponytail and held with a red hairband. Her skin was creamy white and she had freckles on her cheeks. I didn't know Francine's last name, but if it wasn't O'Toole or Murphy or some other Irish name, I'd eat my hat. She was shapely enough, with a trim figure and wide hips that swayed as she walked.

"I hope its extra strong this morning, Francine," I said.

Francine smiled, "Stuck a fork in it myself to check."

She set down two clean cups and poured out the dark black brew. The aroma was invigorating as I grabbed one of the steaming cups.

"Hey, Francine," said Joe. "So, how's my doll this morning?" He cast his eyes over her body, taking her all in, then reached up and patted her on her rear. Francine just grunted at his awkward fondling and went back to the counter.

Joe and I drank our coffee. It was as strong as Francine had promised. For the rest of the breakfast Joe played his game with Francine. George must have given him some bum tips on Francine's likes—which didn't surprise me in the least—since apparently Francine hated Greek food, couldn't stand boxing, and was allergic to cats. Despite Joe's usual failure for the morning, I thought I could see a change in Francine's demeanor; she didn't seem to put her normal venom into her rebuttals of Joe's advances.

After about twenty minutes Joe had received and devoured his flapjacks, so I figured I had done my duty as a friend. The initial jolt from the coffee was starting to ebb and I finally took my leave. I shrugged into my coat and tossed a nickel onto the table to pay for my coffee. The cold morning air had a sharp bite to it, helping to clear some of the cobwebs. As I passed the window outside the diner I was stunned. I saw Francine sit down in the booth across from Joe. *Huh, I guess persistence does pay off.*

It was Saturday morning and there were almost no commuters on the L. The air was crisp and clean, and I could smell a snow storm brewing. The cold air continued to invigorate me as I walked from the L up Racine. I passed a bakery on the way and the aroma of fresh baked bread filled the air. For a brief moment, I thought of picking up some challah for Mom. I even gave a passing thought to surprising them at Temple, but I think that would have given Mom a heart attack. I would have fallen asleep during the service, and that would have embarrassed Dad.

Instead, I continued on to my tenement. I still didn't have any idea of how I was going to get the books from the Feds, but I had a whole night to think about it since I didn't have to go back to work until Sunday evening. I entered my tenement and trudged up the three flights of stairs to my apartment. Mrs. Rabinowitz was thankfully absent, so I was able to make it to my door without any neighborly attention. I put the key in the lock and gave a satisfied nod when it turned with a click. I entered my apartment, turning on the bare light in the kitchen and tossing my coat on top of the coat that was already draped across one of the chairs.

I was heading to my room when I stopped. *Another coat?* I turned back to the kitchen and looked up just as the floor boards creaked. I caught a glimpse of motion right before my face exploded in pain as a hand slammed so hard into my left cheek that my vision blurred.

"You son of a bitch! You left me for dead!"

My face stung, sharp pinpricks of pain darting across my cheek, but it was the sound of her voice that shocked me more. *Moira?* I think my jaw fell open, because I couldn't say anything.

Moira stood before me and I blinked a few times to make sure that it was really her. She looked radiant in a red blouse with pearl-white buttons, black slacks, and black short-heeled shoes. Her green eyes flared. She looked beautiful... and furious. Maybe it wasn't the smart thing to do, but I didn't have anything to say, so I grabbed her and quickly pulled her to me, kissing her deeply on her mouth.

She pushed me away, "Uh, uh. You can't just kiss and make up for this. I was shot and you left me for dead on the frozen fucking street!"

"Moira," I stepped back and held up my hands. I wanted to block any other attempts to slap me. "You were dead! You were covered in blood. There was a bullet through your chest. I even checked you for a pulse and you didn't have one! You were dead!"

"And so, what, you left me there to be food for the jackals?" Her voice was scathing.

"I couldn't stay there with a dead body. The cops were on their way, and I wasn't gonna try to explain to them what happened since I didn't even know myself." I walked past her and into my living room. "Hell, Moira," I held up my hands, "when I didn't see your name listed in the papers along with the other guys that were killed I knew I had made a mistake. I went to every hospital in the city yesterday to see if you had been admitted." I turned around and looked at her. She stood in the entry to the kitchen, her hair backlit by the kitchen bulb. It cast her face in a sensual shadow.

"You mean so much to me," I pleaded, taking a tentative step toward her. "I was devastated. I watched you bleed all over the street, and then I spent what seemed like an endless day visiting hospital after hospital." I took another step. "And with each hospital, when I didn't find you, it only reinforced what I had seen happen to you; that you must have died." I reached out and gently held Moira by the shoulders. She flinched, but didn't pull away. "And now here, you are standing in my apartment, definitely alive," I reached up and touched my cheek, which still stung. "But how?"

She looked at me with her green eyes. I saw anger there, but it was muted and I thought I could see a twinge of regret. "Oh, Saul, I didn't realize what you went through." She grabbed my hands and held them in hers. "Getting shot was so excruciating; I wanted to die the pain was so intense. I guess I fainted from the shock and the pain, but the bullet must have only grazed me. When I came to and you weren't there I was so pissed! Can you imagine what I went through, waking up covered in blood, and not seeing you? I thought something had happened to you as well, there was so much blood on the ground." Moira reached up and stroked my cheek where she had slapped me earlier.

Her touch was like velvet, and a shiver went up my spine. "Moira, I'm so happy that you're alive. Are you sure you're alright?"

"I'm fine," she said as she tilted her head up and kissed me gently on my lips. I kissed her back, my lips pushing against hers, my mouth opening up ever so slightly. I shuddered. Even the French kiss that we'd shared on the day she'd been shot hadn't felt like this. I wasn't a virgin; I'd learned the practicalities of the birds and the bees with a girl in high school, but Moira was special. Her beauty had entranced me from the first day that I saw her in the diner. I had fantasized about her from that moment, but she'd always been a bit distant, insisting that she had wanted to get to know me first.

Now she kissed me harder, her left hand reaching up to caress my head, her right hand sliding down to grab my ass. I embraced her, breaking the kiss and nibbling her lower lip, my left hand reaching up to stroke her breast. A sigh escaped her lips.

I began to maneuver Moira backwards, into the kitchen. As we moved, we continued to kiss, her hands untucking my shirt and tugging at my belt. She paused in the doorway to my bedroom, ripping at my shirt, tearing it open, the buttons popping off. The remains of my shirt dropped to the floor as her hands caressed my chest, tracing a line down to my pants. I managed to kick off my shoes as she pulled my pants down.

I stood there, naked except for my socks. I was excited, and thrilled, and just a bit nervous. Moira pushed me onto the bed. I landed heavily on the quilts and she gave me a little smirk. "I guess you really are Jewish." She slowly unbuttoned her blouse, then let the red fabric fall to the floor to reveal pert, white breasts. With a couple of deft motions she stepped out of her pants. She stood there for a second, the late morning light from the window shining on her gorgeous body.

She climbed onto the bed, kissing me across my chest and neck. I began to caress her silky smooth body, stroking her breasts, returning her kisses. Moira raked her hands across my chest, scratching me with her manicured nails. It hurt, but I was too focused on her body, and what her mouth was doing, to really care.

She sat up, her legs straddling me. I let my hands caress her petite breasts, and she let another sigh escape as she arched her back. She grabbed my hands in hers, pushing them back above my head. She bent down, kissing me on my lips, then my chin, walking the kisses down my throat. She paused on my throat, her teeth nibbling at my skin, then continued down my chest. I sighed as she continued, anticipating her path. Her kisses continued down my stomach, and I gasped, "Oh, yes."

She continued to kiss me. I couldn't be sure, but as she glanced up at me it looked like her eyes flashed red for a moment. *Must be a trick of the light.* Then she bit me on the right side of my stomach. "Ouch!" I yelled, expecting it to hurt more than it did. "Not so hard, honey."

Her only answer was a deep-throated growl as she continued to gnaw on my stomach. I could see blood welling up around her lips. I struggled briefly, but her grip was like iron and I quickly tired. Her head came up, blood encircling her lips. She had a feral, animal-like look in her eyes and her teeth looked longer and sharper than normal. *Another trick of the light?*

Despite her devilish look, I was calm and relieved. This was not what I had expected when I first laid eyes on Moira at the diner. I should have been scared. I should have been in pain. But instead I felt peaceful and amazing, as if this was how life was supposed to be.

Moira bent down and brushed her breast against the wound, letting the nipple dip into the blood and then trace up my chest. She leaned down to kiss me and I could taste my blood on her lips and in her mouth.

She pulled away and placed the bloody nipple before my mouth. I was drunk with lust and I weakly lifted my head to kiss her breast, sucking off the blood. I wanted to continue. I didn't want to disappoint her, but my head was heavy and flopped back onto my pillows. She smiled and let go of my hands, placing her hands on her hips.

"I'm sorry," I managed to croak out. "I guess I'm more tired than I thought."

"It's okay, baby. It happens to a lot of guys." She licked one of the scratches she had made on my chest, then rubbed her bloody tongue against her lips and perfect teeth. She leaned down and gently kissed me again. By this time, my long day yesterday, long work shift, and the emotional shock of finding Moira alive caught up with me. I tried to keep my eyes open as she kissed me again, but my reserves had been used up, and I fell asleep.

Chapter 10

I awoke alone. I didn't remember anything after our love-making—I didn't even remember dreaming. Moira must have pulled up the quilts and laid them over me at some point. It was evening; my room was dark except for a pool of light from the kitchen. I could smell coffee brewing. I smiled. *It's awfully nice of Moira to make me coffee.*

I stretched, and winced in pain. I had forgotten how 'physical' Moira's love-making had been. I pulled up the quilt and looked down at my stomach. I thought it was a little bite, that she had just gotten carried away, but what I saw looked more like I'd been bitten by some wild animal. Blood had congealed around a deep bite mark, and as I gently touched it some blood oozed from the wound. "Man, I like a woman who gets physical, but this is crazy."

I got out of bed and padded to the bathroom, the floorboards cold against my bare feet. I clicked on the light and looked at myself in the mirror. In addition to my 'love bite', I had about two dozen long scratches down my chest. They were red and puffy and dried blood was clinging to a couple of the scratches. "I don't know if I can handle any more love from her," I said to the mirror.

I ran the tap and used a wash cloth to clean up the

scratches and some of the blood around my stomach. The scratches looked red and raw, but at least they weren't still bleeding. The bite on my stomach still bled a little. I couldn't do anything about it; I didn't have any bandages or anything in the apartment. Shrugging, I walked back into the bedroom and pulled on my pants. I found my shirt and put it on, forgetting that half the buttons had been removed when Moira had ripped it off of me.

"Hey, doll," I called out to Moira. "Pour me some of that coffee." I pulled off the shirt and tossed it toward the bathroom, grabbing another shirt from the wardrobe.

I headed to the kitchen, yawning and rubbing my hand through my hair. Instead of Moira, there was a strange man sitting patiently in my favorite kitchen chair. He had a cup of coffee in front of him. I stared at him for a moment, confusion on my face as I tried to figure out who he was and how he'd gotten in. Curious, I walked over to the door and clicked the lock, then tried to open the door. It didn't budge. I shrugged, turned around and sat down in the other chair.

The stranger was about my height, which put him at about 5'8". He had dirty brown hair that was neatly combed and glistened a bit in the light from the kitchen bulb; pomade, I guessed, since it didn't look like Dapper Dan. He had brown eyes that looked at me curiously, like I was some kind of animal on display. He looked young, maybe a year older than me. He was dressed in a dark blue suit, with a white shirt and black tie. The suit looked like it was a little bit too big for him, almost like my bar mitzvah suit fit me. I didn't think that he was somebody from Moran's or Capone's gangs, as they tended to dress a bit snazzier in tailored suits. He was dressed too nicely to be a private dick, but there was an air of cop about him.

"Good evening, Mr. Imbierowicz," he chuckled. "Or should I say good morning." He slid the coffee across the table to me. "I'm assuming you take it black since I found neither milk nor sugar in your kitchen." He sounded apologetic and embarrassed by my lack of groceries.

I didn't say anything, but grabbed the cup and took a drink. I was a bit surprised since my crap coffee actually tasted pretty decent. I wondered what he did to make it taste so good, but I was determined to force him into telling me what was up. I figured it was the least he could do since he'd broken into my apartment.

"I'm Agent Wright, Mr. Imbierowicz," he pulled a wallet from his inside coat pocket and showed me a brass badge. It read BUREAU OF INVESTIGATION. I immediately began to sweat. *Shit, just what I need, the Feds.*

"I think you know why we're here," Agent Wright said. "You have information that we need. If you tell me what I want to know then I can make sure that things go easy for you. If you don't cooperate, then unfortunately I'm authorized to get the information we need by any means necessary."

Man, how could somebody who sounded so polite, be so threatening? I finally recognized his voice as being that of one of the two Feds that I had seen go into the janitor's closet. That meant he was looking for information about Ralph Capone, or he knew that I'd been 'asked' to steal that information for Moran.

"Look, man," I set the coffee down on the table. "I want to help you."

"That's good to know," Agent Wright said.

"But I need to know what you can do to protect my family. I won't tell you anything until I have some assurances that the Feds can keep them safe."

The agent gave me a quizzical look. I plowed on. "Moran knows that you have the books on Ralph. He sent his goons after me the other day and told me to get the books for him. If I don't, my parents are dead." I looked Agent Wright straight in the eyes. "I need to know what you Feds can do to keep my family safe."

"That ain't why we're here, you kike." The raspy, gruff voice came from the living room. Surprised, I bristled at the derogatory name and leaned my chair back to look in that direction as the floor lamp was clicked on. A heavyset, bear of a man sat on my couch. He wore a similar suit to that of Agent Wright, though his was even more ill-fitting; tight around his wide neck and belly. The left side of his face and neck was scarred. He held my only glass with the dregs of some coffee in it. "Where's your bitch at?"

I could see Agent Wright's face redden out of the corner of my eye. "You mean Moira?" I asked. Yeah—I know he couldn't be talking about anybody else, but I was a bit shocked. *Why would the Feds care about my girlfriend?*

"Yeah, I'm talking about your fuckin' dame," Gruff said. He rose off the couch and walked toward the kitchen. "That *kurva* bitch you *shtuped* earlier today."

He stood in the doorway to the living room. I must admit I found his Yiddish to be pretty flawless, though I didn't like him calling Moira a whore. I know she bit me, but when you're in love you tend to overlook those things. "Hey, what gives you the right to call Moira that?" I rose from my chair. "And what the hell does she have to

64

do with this?"

Gruff laughed, a gravely sound. Agent Wright said, "Look, Saul—can I call you Saul? You know why Special Agent Truesdale and I need to see Moira. She came to us with information, but then she backed out on her promise to help us."

"Nobody breaks a promise to the Feds," Agent Truesdale said.

"What in the hell are you talking about?" I was flabbergasted. These two had to be pulling some sort of joke on me. "Why would Moira need to come to you in the first place? And even if she did, she'd never break any promise that she's made."

Agent Truesdale finished off his coffee and set the glass down on the counter. "Listen, jerk. That dame is dangerous." He pointed at the scratches on my chest, visible through the unbuttoned part of my shirt. "You should be more careful. She'll chew you up and spit you out."

I involuntarily reached down and touched my bite wound. *Man, was that an accurate statement.*

"Tell us where she went," Agent Wright said leaning forward. He actually sounded like he was pleading. "Help us out, otherwise we can't guarantee your safety. Or that of your family."

I had had enough. I was tired of people just waltzing into my apartment whenever they damn well pleased, and here these two jokers were talking nonsense about Moira. I might have been afraid to stand up to Moran's goons, but I wasn't going to let the Feds push me around as well.

"I don't know where Moira is." I said, letting my voice rise. "And even if I did, I certainly wouldn't turn her over to the damn Feds." I pointed at Truesdale. "Especially a fat *momzer* like you."

"Wrong answer, pretty-boy."

I never saw the punch that came from my right. Truesdale's massive fist hit me across the jaw and actually spun me toward the table. I blacked out before I hit the floor. In retrospect, maybe calling him a bastard wasn't such a good idea.

Chapter 11

When I came to, I was lying on my kitchen floor. As I stood up the room began spinning, so I grabbed the chair to support myself. I shakily managed to sit down, resting my elbows on the table and cradling my aching head. Even though my head felt like the L had run over it, at least it made me forget about the pain in my stomach. Once the carousel that was my kitchen stopped turning, I stood up and went over to the icebox to find something cold to put on my very swollen cheek.

To my surprise, I saw a package of hamburger was nestled within the glacier that was taking over the icebox. I was briefly taken aback by the sudden image of my stomach wound and how much it looked like the chopped steak down at Mr. Holtz's butcher shop. I shook my head to banish the thought, which caused the carousel to take a few more turns. I steadied myself against the icebox and managed to pull the hamburger out, pressing it gently against my cheek. As the frozen meat worked its magic my mind slowly cleared. *Where did I get hamburger from?* I realized that Mom must have brought it by the other day since I couldn't remember the last time that I'd been to the butcher's. I doubt any of my other recent guests would have been kind enough to leave me such a thoughtful gift.

Once I sat back down, I noticed a folded scrap of paper sitting on the table. It looked like it had been torn from a stenographer's pad. I unfolded it and at the top, printed in a careless and harsh hand that had to belong to Special Agent Truesdale, was written:

Find the dame and bring her to us or I'll even out your face. We'll be watching.

A post script was written at the bottom of the page in a neat, scholarly penmanship:

Thank you for the coffee.

~ Agent Wright.

The note was insult added to injury. I crumpled it up and tossed it into the sink. My head was hurting and it wasn't just from its encounter with Truesdale's fist. Three days ago my life had been pretty normal. I had a decent job and a beautiful girlfriend. Since then my life had been turned upside down. "I think I'm starting to hate Valentine's Day," I said to the empty room.

Once my face was finally numb from the cold of the now semi-thawed hamburger, I tossed it back into the icebox. Despite being unconscious for I don't know how long, I was exhausted. I checked the lock again; I was starting to think that Mrs. Rabinowitz was right about getting a second one. I turned off the light and headed to my bedroom.

I climbed into bed, trying to figure out what I was

going to do next. I now had Bugs Moran *and* the Feds after me. I suppose I should consider myself lucky that at least they each wanted something different from me.

Moran wanted me to get the damn books from the Feds so that he could make sure that Capone didn't get them. That would give Moran some leverage against Capone. I definitely didn't like the thought of being a part of a change in the balance of gangland power in Chicago. Being caught between the two biggest crime bosses in the city seemed like a very dangerous place to be.

On top of that, I didn't know what the hell the Feds wanted with Moira. *Why'd they come to me looking for her? If they knew that she was here, why didn't they come earlier to talk with her? For that matter, why didn't they go to her place? They're the Feds, so they have to know where she lives, even if I don't. Besides, what information could Moira have that the Feds would want?*

I guess I had to admit to myself that I really didn't know all that much about Moira. In addition to not knowing where she lived, I didn't even know what she did when she wasn't with me. She had to have some money, her clothes were too nice, and she always seemed to want to go to swanky places. I didn't think she actually had a job—she'd never mentioned one— and she'd always been flexible with my schedule, so I figured that she never had to be anyplace in the morning to get to work.

So what could the Feds want with her? Did they want to know about the gunfight on Valentine's Day and why we had both been there? But if that's what they wanted, why didn't they ask me about it? And why would the Feds even care about one gang killing some guys from a rival gang? That was more of a police matter, not anything of interest for the Feds. Sure, there had been talk and such about getting Capone and trying to clean up the city, but the Feds usually didn't give a crap about the rank and file gangsters.

As I lay under the quilts, my mind wandered back to Valentine's Day morning. *Why did Moira ask me to meet her so far north from our usual place? Did she live in that area and wanted to meet somewhere close to her place?* When we had left the diner Moira had insisted we walk toward the garage where the murders took place. *Was that a coincidence? Was her place near the garage?*

Suddenly, a new thought struck me —*could Moira have known about the gang hit?* I laughed it off almost as soon as I thought of it. That was such a preposterous idea that I couldn't seriously consider it. Sure, the hit had to have been planned by somebody. You don't just stroll into a garage armed with machine guns without having planned on using them. It was too far-fetched to think that Moira was even remotely connected to the massacre.

As I started to drift off to sleep, my thoughts circled back to the Feds and Moran. I didn't like the Feds; they seemed like a pair of cock-sure asses, but I wasn't scared of them. They wouldn't do anything to my family if I failed to help them out. Moran, however, scared the shit out of me. He was the one I needed to keep happy. But if I could do that *and* help the Feds at the same time...

I figured that the simplest thing to do was to convince Moira to help me out. I could tell the Feds that Moira and I would talk to them, but only on the condition that they give me the books, which I could then give to Moran. *Simple.*

The way that things had been going, though, I wasn't

going to hold my breath. None of this could happen until I found Moira.

Chapter 12

It was actually morning when I woke up on Sunday. Weak winter sunlight trickled in through my bedroom window. I lay in bed for a few minutes, listening. I couldn't hear anything to make me think that there was someone else in my apartment, and I didn't smell any coffee. Just to be sure, I called out, "Hello? Who's there?" but nobody answered. "What, no visitors? I'm *verklempt.*"

I finally got out of bed and went to the bathroom. After relieving myself, I checked my various wounds. The right side of my face was bruised and slightly swollen, but not too badly. The scratches on my chest looked okay. They appeared to be superficial and most had already started to heal.

My 'love bite' wasn't doing so well. It was tender and bruised, and it was still oozing fresh blood. Despite my feelings for Moira, and the great sex, I was concerned by the wound. "Next time I'll have to show *her* who's in charge."

I opened the medicine cabinet looking for a bottle of iodine, thinking that maybe Mom had left some on one of her many visits, but I didn't see anything. I grabbed the washcloth and soap and gingerly cleaned the bite. Blood sluiced off and I winced at the pain. After a couple of minutes I managed to clean most of the bite. I thought about going to my parent's house; I knew that Mom would have some iodine, but I *also* knew that she'd pester me with questions that I just wasn't ready to answer.

I finished up in the bathroom and went into the kitchen to make some coffee. As I dumped the coffee grounds into the pot, I wondered what the Feds had done to make such good Joe. I had never brewed a pot so good. Despite their arrogance, I wished that they had told me what they had done to get such a good brew.

I finished brewing the coffee and cleaned the cup that Agent Wright had used last night. I filled the cup and grimaced at the first sip. "Must be a government secret," I concluded.

I gave up on the coffee and poured the rest of the cup out into the sink. I was planning to head out to look for Moira, so I figured I'd start at the diner at work since that was where we had met. If nothing else, I'd be able to get a decent cup of Joe and something to eat there.

I finished getting dressed, left, and locked the apartment. I paused outside my door and tried the handle a few times, pushing the door and twisting the knob. It didn't budge. I sighed and headed down the stairs.

I walked past Mrs. Rabinowitz's door and wasn't surprised when it quickly opened. "Good morning, Saul," she called to me.

I briefly thought about ignoring her, but my mother had raised me better than that. I stopped and smiled at her. "Hello, Mrs. R. How are you this morning?"

"Goodness gracious, Saul," she exclaimed. "What happened to you?"

I unconsciously reached for my stomach before I realized that she was talking about my face. I had already forgotten about the bruise. "I slipped in the bath," I lied.

She looked at me with a critical eye, but then seemed to decide that what had actually happened didn't really matter.

"Your lady friend is quite nice looking," she said, changing the subject. "You should invite her over for tea someday."

"Thank you, " I said. "I'll do that." I could tell she was fishing for information. It didn't surprise me; Mrs. R. had been a true busybody since the day I had moved in. But in this case, I was pretty sure she was fishing on my Mom's behalf. I had casually mentioned Moira to Mom the day after I had met her. Since then, she'd been trying to find out as much as she could about Moira. *Unlike me, apparently.* Mom would have preferred that I find a nice Jewish gal from the neighborhood, like Melissa Adamovicz, and she was looking for any opportunity to find Moira's flaws and weaknesses so that she could parade them before me. Mrs. Rabinowitz was a willing accomplice in gathering this information.

"She does keep strange hours doesn't she?"

"Hmm?" Now I was curious. *Did Mrs. R. know something that could be useful to me?*

"Well, she left your place so late in the afternoon the other day. Such an odd time of the day to be heading out. Well, that is to be leaving without you, of course. It's probably a normal time for a couple to head out for going to dinner or something, but she left without you, so that was strange. And she headed out in weather like this without a coat. You should tell her she'll catch her death."

I sighed. She was almost as bad as Joe. "There's nothing weird about her leaving in the afternoon. We spent the day talking and since I work nights I was ready to go to sleep. It would be very imprudent of her to stay while I was sleeping." I smiled at my ingenuity. I had managed to answer Mrs. Rabinowitz's question in such a way to make me seem like the height of purity and innocence with my girlfriend.

"Well, that's nice to know. But why did she come back later?"

Wait, what? "She came back later? When?"

"It was last night." She paused in thought. "Though apparently she didn't stay long as she left just a few minutes after arriving. Did the two of you get into a scuffle? It looked like her lips were bleeding."

"No, of course not." I was confused. *Was I so out of it last night that I didn't remember Moira coming by? Why would she come by and not wake me up? Mrs. Rabinowitz must be wrong.*

"Look, Mrs. R. I need to go meet my parents."

"Of course, dear. You're such a good son." She waved as I turned to head down the stairs. "Say hello to your mother for me."

Chapter 13

Outside it was cold, but sunny, with only a slight breeze coming in off Lake Michigan. I turned up the collar on my coat and pulled my hat down as far as it would go. *Why would Moira come back and not tell me?* I was confused, and the only way to find the answers was to find Moira.

We had first met at the diner at the Post Office and she had continued to meet me there every morning except for St. Valentine's Day. She'd only come back to my apartment once, and we had met one time for drinks at that speakeasy. I had never been to her place and I didn't even know in which part of town she lived. She had always wanted to talk about me, and to be honest, I was really only interested in trying to get into her pants. As long as she came to me, I never bothered to learn where she spent the rest of her time.

As I walked to the L, I wracked my brain to try to remember if Moira had ever said anything about where she lived, or even just a place where she hung out. I thought back to our first meeting at the diner. I had just gotten off of my shift and Joe and I had gone down to the diner for breakfast. I was still getting used to working the night shift and chatting with Joe was helping me to get into the routine. The booths had been full that day, so Joe and I had sat at the counter.

Right after I sat down a woman's voice asked me, "Is this seat taken?"

"No," I said. I caught a glimpse out of the corner of my eye and turned to look at her, a wolfish grin on my face. As I finally got a good look at her, I was stunned. She was the most beautiful person that I had ever laid eyes on. Her skin was a pale alabaster, with a little color on the cheeks and full, red lips. She was wearing a low-cut sky blue blouse with a matching skirt and a long string of pearls. Perched on top of flaming red hair was a white cloche hat with blue trim decorated with tiny blue flowers. She was dressed like she was ready to go out on the town.

She pulled a cigarette out of a mother-of-pearl case and tapped it twice. "Do you have a light?" Her voice was sultry.

In reply, I pulled out my Ronson and lit her cigarette.

"Thanks...," she paused, prompting me.

"Saul." I smiled at her. "You're welcome..." I returned the favor.

"Moira." She took a pull on her cigarette. "I do love a man who's helpful and polite." She smiled at me, revealing perfect teeth.

"I'm always happy to help a beautiful lady." I know it wasn't the best pick-up line in the history of the world, but give a guy a break. I had just gotten off of a 10-hour shift.

"You must be new around here," she stated as Francine poured her a cup of coffee. "I usually come in a couple times a week after a long night, and I think I would have remembered seeing you before." She gave me a small smile.

"I just started a few days ago," I said. "And I know I

would have remembered seeing *you* before."

"Well, I'm glad I decided to stop in this morning." She reached out and lightly touched my arm. An almost electric shock ran through me. "Had I gone straight home, I would have missed meeting you." Her smile warmed.

"Do you live nearby?" I asked, not really caring. I was trying to make small talk so that she'd stay around. My plan was to offer to walk her home and see what developed.

"I get around." She took a sip of coffee. "What about you? Do you like working for the Post Office?"

"It's pretty good so far," I shrugged, feeling that I needed to say more. "It's allowed me to meet some 'interesting' people." I nodded toward Joe. I tried to give her my best smile. My heart skipped a beat when she smiled back.

"So what do you do when you aren't delivering mail?" She ran a manicured finger around the rim of her coffee cup.

"I don't *actually* deliver the mail. I work up on the third floor in the sorting room. It's not the most glamorous job in the world, but it has to get done." She looked at me expectantly, her green eyes seeming to bore into me as I realized I hadn't actually answered her question. "Well, not much really. I like to go out dancing, and having the occasional drink."

She laughed, "So I guess that means you aren't dry."

"Heck, who is these days?" I laughed as well. "You know, you and I could go out some night for a drink."

"Are you asking me on a date, Saul?" She smiled coyly at me. "Are you always this forward with women?"

"Well....I mean...uh..." I stammered, and I could feel my face turning red.

"Slick move, man," Joe laughed at my expense.

Moira took a pull on her cigarette. "I like a man who takes charge of things." She gave me a wink. Joe's laughter stopped and he mumbled something about "of all the luck" as he got up from his stool and headed out of the diner.

"We should get together tonight," Moira suggested.

"Uh," I hesitated. I had to work tonight and I knew that if I missed work I would be out of a job, but I also didn't want Moira to think that I was a *nebish*. "I can go out for a bit, but I have to be at work by ten." *There—an almost perfect balance of commitment and refusal.*

"Have you heard of the Green Mill Lounge?"

"Over on Broadway?" I asked.

Moira nodded. "Meet me there tonight at seven." She patted my hand and got up from her stool, crushing out her cigarette before she headed for the door. I stared after her, watching her gams as she strode across the diner. I turned in my stool to follow her path out the door as she turned and headed up the street.

Francine stuck a napkin in my face. I look at her quizzically. "To clean up the drool, hon."

I snapped out of my reverie as the L stopped at Canal. I got off the train and headed out of the station. I was thinking that I would start my search at the Green Mill, the speakeasy we went to on our first date, but I knew that they wouldn't be open until later in the evening. I guess I should have thought this through more before leaving my apartment, but the smell of fresh-brewed coffee coming from the diner reminded me why I had left early.

I walked into the diner and sat at the counter. The

place looked different in the day. I was used to the bright lights at night; the diner was a shining beacon in the dark. The muted daylight spilling in through grimy windows made the place look run down. The light seemed to accentuate the nicks in the countertop, the tears in the seats, and the stains on the floor.

"Aren't you a little early for work, hon?"

I looked up at Francine. I didn't realize that she worked this late in the day, or on Sundays for that matter. "Sometimes a creature of the night wants to see what life is like during the day."

She smiled and automatically poured me a cup of coffee. "Looks like you had a rough time of it last night." She pointed to my bruised cheek with the coffee pot.

"You should see the other guy." I smiled and picked up the cup. As Francine turned away, I called after her. "Hey, Francine?" She stopped and leaned on the counter, probably because business was slow at this time of the day. Francine was nice enough, but in the mornings she was always busy. It was one of the reasons she gave Joe such a hard time for harassing her. "Do you know the dame that I met here and have hung out with for the past week?"

Francine turned her pretty blue eyes up toward the ceiling in thought. After a moment, she looked back at me and slowly nodded her head. "Yeah, that pretty redhead with the green eyes. She always looks like she's just come from a night on the town."

"Do you know anything about her?"

"What do you mean?"

"Oh, nothing," I said quickly. "I just wanted to talk to her and I don't know where she lives. I was hoping you might know something." *Why did I feel ashamed for asking about Moira? Wasn't it common for a guy to want to find out secrets about the woman he loves? Of course, most gals probably don't keep where they live a secret from their boyfriends.*

Francine gave me a quizzical look, and then shrugged slightly. "Sorry, hon." She gave me a sympathetic smile. "I wish I could help you, but I don't think I ever saw her come in before you started working here. Besides, I'm usually too busy in the mornings to really pay any attention to what goes on outside the diner."

Another customer sat down at the end of the counter. Francine patted my hand and left to take his order. I sat and drank my coffee, brooding. It had been a long shot that Francine would have known anything. *I could ask the cook,* I thought, *but he sees even less of what goes on in the diner than Francine does.*

I finished my coffee and pulled out a nickel and put it on the counter. I gave Francine my thanks and told her that I'd see her in the morning; I then headed back outside.

A cold wind had picked up and was blowing in off the lake. I pulled up my collar and shoved my hands deep into my pockets. Despite the cold, there were a lot of people out on the street. I turned toward Michigan Avenue and away from the L. I wasn't sure what I was going to do, but the cold air felt good and it helped to clear my head. I thought back to the morning of Valentine's Day. *Why did Moira insist on meeting her up north? Maybe she lived up there?* It was another long shot, but I was getting desperate. I turned and headed north.

Chapter 14

I walked up Michigan Avenue and wandered through Lincoln Park. Despite the cold and wind there were a lot of people out enjoying the sunshine this Sunday. I still wasn't sure where to start looking for Moira or where she lived. This was nothing more than a shot in the dark. I started thinking that this search was hopeless before I had even started looking. I was seriously considering just forgetting about it and heading to my parents for dinner.

How would I even try to find where Moira lived? Should I go up to every building in the neighborhood and ask people if a Moira lived there? It's not like I had a picture of her to show anyone, and I'm sure that if I started asking questions to complete strangers I'd be lucky to just get a door slammed in my face.

Who am I kidding? I thought to myself. It was stupid of me to even think that I could try to find Moira.

I stopped in frustration and anger at myself for being so stupid, ready to give up the search. As I looked around, I noticed that the building I had stopped in front of was the SMC Cartage Co, the site of the massacre. I hadn't intended to end up here; I think I would have avoided the place had I been consciously thinking about it. But, as I looked at the plain brick front and the awning over the large front window, I was struck with an urgent curiosity. I had been so close on the day of the killings, and my life had been turned upside down since then, so I felt a need to see the place that, in my mind, had changed my life.

I walked up to the entrance and looked in through the window. There was a short entryway with an open door just inside. Through the doorway I could see a door that presumably led to the back of the building and what looked like an office through another door on the left. I knew from the newspaper photos that the murders had taken place in the back of the building. I put my hand on the door knob and turned it, expecting it to be locked.

Had it been locked, that would have been enough to have blunted my curiosity, but the door opened as I turned on the knob. I was stunned for a moment. I idly wondered why the building wasn't locked, then looked up and down the street to see if anybody was watching. Nobody was too close and so, without a second thought, I entered the building and quickly closed the door behind me.

My heart was racing and my stomach was doing somersaults. I guess I had just committed a crime—breaking into the building—but I let this thought go. I was here, and I had already come this far, so I might as well see the scene of the massacre.

I walked quickly through the reception area and opened the rear door, stepping into the garage in back. The room was dark with the only light coming in from the windows on the garage doors at the back of the building. I closed the door behind me and stood motionless for a moment. After a few seconds my eyes adjusted to the light and I could start to make out details.

Half a dozen cars and trucks were parked in front of me. I sidled between a couple of trucks at the front of the garage and headed toward the back of the building. I walked past a Ford Coupe and a couple of sedans parked against the right wall when I got to the spot I recognized from the photos. The space was relatively empty, just some chairs along the wall to my left, and a table and some shelves on the wall opposite where I stood. There were saws and other tools hanging from the left wall at the far end. The room had a peculiar odor. It was a mixture of dirt, motor oil, and something else I couldn't quite place. It sort of reminded me of Mr. Holtz's butcher shop.

As my eyes continued to adjust to the light, I could see that the wall on my left had several chips and holes in the brickwork from where the bullets had hit. I walked over and reached out with my right hand, touching one of the bullet holes. I recalled that the papers had said that 70 shell casings and some spent shotgun shells had been recovered from the scene. I tried to imagine what it must have been like, the sound of the Tommy Guns clattering away in the garage, the bullets hitting flesh and brick. A shiver ran up my spine at the thought of the noise and destruction and I looked down.

I could see several bloodstains on the floor, some marking small trails where the blood had flowed across the floor. I was standing in a large bloodstain and I involuntarily jumped out of it even though the rational part of my mind knew there was no pool of blood there now.

I immediately recalled all the blood that had covered the frozen sidewalk when Moira had been shot. I could feel the bile rising in my throat. *Why did I come in here? What had I hoped to see?* There was nothing in here that would help me find Moira, or help me out of my predicament.

In disgust I turned to head out of the garage but froze in my tracks. The door at the front of the garage was now open and I could see a body silhouetted in the doorway. I moved to my right, out of sight of the door. *Who could it be?* I thought, carelessly. *Hell, I'm the one that wasn't supposed to be here.* It was probably the owner of the garage, or maybe the cops, coming to investigate a report that somebody had snuck into the place. Either way, I didn't want to be seen.

I heard the creak of the door being closed and a voice, "I still dunno why youse wanna to see da place. Wasn't da pictures in da papers enough?"

Shit! I panicked. I looked around frantically, searching for someplace to hide. I thought about hiding under one of the cars, but they would be sure to see me. I saw several boxes stacked behind one of the sedans along the right wall and ran for them. I managed to jump behind them, sliding to the floor just as the lights to the garage were flicked on.

"If your brothers had been killed wouldn't you want to see where it had happened?" A second voice. The first one had been nasally; this one had sounded a deep bass. I heard footsteps enter the garage and I tried to squeeze myself into as small of a space as I could.

"I suppose," said the first voice. "So, youse was related to some of d'ese guys dat got whacked?"

There was a pause, then the second voice said, "In a manner of speaking."

"Well, whatever. Mr. Moran said to let youse look around all youse wanted."

Shit! They were with Moran! *What are they doing here?* I needed to disappear. If they found me here word would certainly get back to Moran, and I didn't want to know how Bugs would react. The first guy sounded like one of Moran's flunkies, but the second guy sounded like he was from someplace other than Chicago. He'd called the victims 'brothers', but something nagged in the back of my mind that he really didn't mean that they were blood relations.

I could hear a hand rubbing at an unshaven face and then the first voice spoke again. "So, who was yur brudders? I thought everybody dat died here was part of Moran's outfit, ceptin' da doc and da mechanic."

"Schwimmer and May were both brothers. And the Gusenbergs were completing their rites to become brothers as well. Had they completed the process then Frank might have survived."

I was trying to figure out what he meant by that. He was talking like they were all members of some club or fraternity, like the Masons or something. But I wasn't sure how becoming a Mason could have saved anyone from getting shot. Hell, Dad was a member of B'nai B'rith but I don't think they had given Dad any special healing powers. Maybe the Masons—or whatever club he was talking about—were different. There were all sorts of strange stories about the Masons so you could never be sure.

I heard footsteps walking toward me across the garage floor. I tried to make myself even smaller. There was a long whistle, and the first voice said, "Shit, I guess if youse put enough bullets into anything even youse guys can be killed." There was a chuckle that was abruptly cut off by a choking sound. My curiosity got the better of me and I risked a peek around the boxes.

In the harsh light of the bare light bulbs I saw the strangest thing I'd ever seen in my life. Standing near the bullet-pocked north wall was a tall man, at least six-three or more in height, with broad shoulders and a thin, wiry body. He had very pale skin and short-cut brown hair. He was dressed in brown slacks and brown shoes, with a long brown leather coat. *Man, this guy has a thing for brown.* I think even his shirt was a light brown color. That wasn't the unusual thing though. I'd seen plenty of guys that looked like him, but minus the fetish for the color brown. No, what was odd was that Mr. Brown was holding the other guy by the throat with one hand, and he was holding him at least two feet off the floor! Moran's man was pudgy—heck, he was fat—he must have been about 250 pounds, and dressed in the usual baggy, dark-colored suit that Moran must get in bulk from Sears. His trench coat was open, as was his suit jacket, and I could see the heel of a handgun sitting in a shoulder holster. He wasn't reaching for the gun, probably because he was using both hands in an attempt to pry Mr. Brown's hand from his throat.

The goon's feet were flailing about, trying to kick Mr. Brown or to find some purchase on the floor. He was slowly turning blue in the face and was making sputtering sounds.

Mr. Brown just held him there with his right arm locked tight. "Yes, even we can be killed. We've been killed for centuries. And if my brother's deaths are an amusement to you then I will be happy to let you join them." He casually flung the man—like he was tossing a rag doll—right toward me! *Shit!*

Moran's man hit the ground and slid into the boxes,

causing them to tumble and fall to the floor. I sat there, crouched, my hands flung up to protect my head from the falling boxes, and stared up at Mr. Brown, who was looking quite surprised to see me.

"Who the fuck are you?" Mr. Brown yelled.

"Ummm..."

Okay, not the most impressive of responses. I suppose that, had I not been scared shitless, I might have been able to come up with something better to say. You try coming up with witty responses in the heat of the moment. It's not that easy.

Mr. Brown took a step toward me, and I did the only thing I could. I pushed a box toward him and bolted toward the back of the garage. I was hoping to get out the door to the alley and make my escape.

A blur of movement came from my right and suddenly Mr. Brown was standing right in front of me, blocking the exit. *How the fuck did he get there?*

I skidded to a halt and fell flat on my ass, looking up at Mr. Brown. He towered over me and gave me a wicked, toothy grin—man, were his canines really long—and reached down to grab me. I scrambled backwards, trying to crab-walk out of his grasp, but he was faster and grabbed me by the throat. With seemingly no effort at all he lifted me off the ground. I quickly found my throat being squeezed, unable to breathe.

His hand—I think he was just using his left hand—felt like an iron vice. I clawed at his hand, trying to get it to open, but it didn't budge. My vision was beginning to fade.

"Whoever you are, maybe a light snack is in order."

I was starting to lose consciousness, so I wasn't sure if I'd heard him right. *Snack? How could I eat anything if he was choking me?*

I felt his breath on my neck. *What is he doing? Is he trying to kiss me or something?*

There was a sharp intake of breath from Mr. Brown and he suddenly let me go. I dropped to the floor and lay gasping for breath, reaching up to gingerly massage my throat.

"Who are you?" Mr. Brown asked, pointing an accusing finger at me.

"I'm nobody," I managed to rasp out through my aching throat. "Pleasure to meet you." *There, something witty.*

"So, you're the one." Mr. Brown stood up and smoothed down his leather coat.

What the hell is he talking about? "Yup, I'm the one," I managed to say. "Sure, that's me." I started to crawl away from him, but my back hit the wall.

"What kind of game is she playing at?" Mr. Brown turned away and walked back to the main garage. He reached down and picked up Moran's man, who had been gasping for breath on the floor among the boxes. He got the man to stand on his own and even dusted him off. He then picked up a pair of fedoras that had apparently fallen off during their altercation and placed one on Moran's man, then placed the other—also brown with a brown leather band—*what is it with this guy and the color brown?*—on his own head.

Mr. Brown turned toward me. "See you around, Saul." He grabbed the goon by the arm and the pair of them walked to the front of the garage. I heard the front door close.

I managed to stand up and walked over to the boxes, where my own cloth cap had fallen. I picked it up and hit it a couple of times against my leg to knock the dust off. *What the hell had just happened?* I was a goner for sure but then Mr. Brown had just stopped and let me go. *Why?* Something about me had made him stop, but I had no idea what it was. And who was he referring to when he'd said, 'What kind of game is *she* playing at'?

I walked toward the back of the garage. Mr. Brown had said that he'd see me around, but I didn't want to take the chance that he meant that he was waiting for me right outside the front door. I headed out into the alley and turned south. I had had enough of the North Side.

Chapter 15

I headed south and west, ending up at the Sedgwick L station. It seemed like a lifetime ago that I'd met Moira here and my life as I'd known it had ended. I climbed the steps to the platform, weary from my recent encounter, and waited for the train.

I took the L over to Western, letting the rocking motion gently lull me into a sort of half-sleep. I'm sure I was quite a sight to look at but I didn't give a damn anymore. I managed to wake up at the right stop and walked toward Douglas Park. It was late afternoon as I walked toward the tenement where my parent's apartment was located. The building was red-brick, four stories tall, and surrounded by similar buildings on the left and right. I felt at home in the old neighborhood. I was happy to be on my own, but walking down the street and hearing people call to each other in Yiddish was comforting. Despite the cold, women were out on their front stoops, gossiping and catching up on the news of the neighborhood. I saw several people I knew and waved greetings to a few of my friends and parents of friends.

I reached my parents place and walked up to the second floor. My mouth began to water as I could smell *knishes* cooking from within. I was about to knock on the door when it was jerked open. I stood there, my hand raised to knock, and looked down at my mother. She stood barely over five feet in height, and was a bit plump. (Hey—you try to find a polite way to say that your mom is fat.)

"You need an invitation to visit your father and me? You move out on your own and suddenly you forget where your parents struggled for years to raise you? You don't call. You don't write. You don't come to Temple." She turned from the door and headed for the small kitchen. "I have to learn how you are doing from your nice neighbor, Mrs. Rabinowitz. At least she keeps an eye on you for me. Otherwise, I wouldn't know anything about what was going on in your life. I don't even know if you are still seeing that pretty red-headed girl or if you got that package of hamburger that your father was good enough to get for you from work."

I tuned Mom out, and headed into the living room where Dad was sitting by the radio. I knew Mom wouldn't care whether I had heard her or not. Hell, I don't think she really expected me to talk to her at all; I was just a new subject for her perpetual commentary on life in the neighborhood.

"Hey, Pop," I took off my coat and hat and tossed them on the back of a chair, then sat down on the couch. Dad was listening to some music program and he leaned over and turned down the volume on the radio.

"Look what the cat dragged in." Dad did a double take as he looked at me. "And it looks like the cat gave you a good smack or three, too. What happened to you, Saul?"

"*Gornisht.* I slipped on a patch of ice." I can lie easily to my parents—I had been doing it since I had been about 7 years old. It doesn't mean that I liked doing it, but when I needed a good cover story I didn't hesitate to bring out a good lie.

"Mmm Hmm. And why do you lie to your father?"

Okay—I said I could easily lie. I didn't say I was very good at it. "It's really nothing, Pop. Just a bit of fun."

"Fun? Looking like you went a round with Jack Dempsey is called fun?" Dad laughed and looked up at the ceiling, "*Oy vay*! God. Please forgive my son. It's clear he doesn't know what he is doing."

I laughed, hoping Dad didn't know how close to the truth that comment was.

"Hey, *nudnik*." My sister Sarah leaned against the door jamb and crossed her arms. Sarah was five years younger than me, and probably dying even more than I had been to get out from under the rule of our parents. Sarah wanted to be like Clara Bow and all the other Hollywood stars, and dressed the part whenever Mom let her.

"Hey, *shlimazl*," I said. Sarah stuck her tongue out at me in response. She didn't like being called a born loser any more than I liked being called a bore, but the nickname fit. She always seemed to get caught whenever she tried to do something sneaky, while I usually got away with it—my earlier lie notwithstanding.

"Go help your mother," Dad said to Sarah.

"Why?" Sarah whined. "I just got here. Besides, Ma always complains when I try to help her in the kitchen."

"Sarah." Dad pointed to the kitchen. Sarah pouted, but she headed out of the room.

"So what do you want, Dad?" I asked. I was just as good at reading his actions as he was at reading mine.

Dad eased himself out of his chair and walked over to the book case. "What, I need a reason to talk to my son?" He pulled out a book and opened it up, pulling out a hip flask from within the hidden space. I knew Dad kept a flask of whiskey hidden in a copy of *The Great Gatsby* that he had put to better use. I knew because I'd sneaked a few nips of the bootleg whiskey myself from time to time. He took a swig and then handed the flask to me.

"No, you don't," I took a sip. The hard liquor burned my throat and I stifled a cough. "Geez, Dad, where did you get this *kaker*?"

Dad took the flask and capped it, putting it back in the book. "A guy I know at work knows some people." Dad shrugged, as if to say, 'what are you going to do?'

"You bring out the good stuff like this, I know it's serious." I grinned as Dad returned to his chair.

"What have you gotten yourself into, Saul?" His voice was quiet, but full of concern.

"Nothing, Dad." I tried to sound confident.

"Don't lie to me, Saul. You've gotten yourself into some sort of mess. This I know." He pointed a finger at me. "Some guys came down to the packing plant, poking around, asking questions about me. They weren't the usual *schlemiels*, you know, from the South Side."

I nodded, a sinking feeling in my stomach telling me where this was going.

"One of the guys said they were from the North Side, members of Moran's gang." Dad looked at me. "What have you done Saul, getting involved with a bunch of thugs and killers? And don't tell me it's nothing. I'm your father. I know you think you can handle this, but you can't." His voice was rising and he had to force himself to keep quiet. Obviously, Mom and Sarah didn't know what was going on and he wanted to keep it that way. "Listen, Saul, I don't know what you are doing, but these guys mean business."

"Did they threaten you?" No sense in trying to deny any of this now. Dad didn't know exactly what was going on, but he that knew something was up.

Dad waved at me in denial. "Nah. They were poking around, asking when I worked, where I lived. But these guys were real *yolds*. A couple of North Siders out of their territory, asking questions of a bunch of Jews and Italians who know who runs this side of Chicago."

Dad sounded proud, but I was still concerned. "Look, Dad, just because nobody talked doesn't mean these guys didn't get what they wanted."

"Bah. They didn't, but you're right. They will eventually." He rubbed his hand over his face. "Tell me what happened. I'll speak to Albert at work. He can help you out."

I knew that Albert was Alberto Corzetti, the head of the meat packer's labor union at the plant. Everybody knew that the unions were in close with the gangs, if not outright run by them. My thoughts leaned to the latter. It was tempting to run to Dad to have him fix my problems, but this would effectively be running to Al Capone, just the man I didn't want to get involved.

"Look, Dad, there's some stuff going on, but it's no big deal. I can handle it."

"You can handle it?" Dad gave me a skeptical look. "You got that shiner on your face and that bruise on your neck by 'handling it'?"

"Yes." I insisted. I had to give Dad something. "A couple of days ago I was near the garage where Moran's men were killed."

"What?" Dad yelled.

"What's that, David?" Mom called from the kitchen.

"Nothing, Miriam."

"Don't tell me it's nothing. That sounded like something."

"If I say it's nothing, it's nothing. Go back to your cooking." Dad glared at me and spoke in a loud whisper. "You were at the massacre? Oy."

"No—I wasn't *at* the massacre." I wasn't about to tell Dad what had happened to me just an hour ago. He'd go nuts if he knew that I'd been in the actual building. "But I was in the street and saw the car drive away. I guess Moran wants to know if I saw anything."

"So why are they nosing around the packing plant? Moran's gotta know that you don't work there. Why doesn't he come to your work?"

"I don't know. A couple of his guys came by on Friday and asked me if I saw anything. I told them I didn't."

"And they didn't believe you? Doesn't this Moran know that my son is no liar?"

Dad was starting to get mad, which was both good and bad. Good, since it was distracting him from the real issue. Bad, because I was afraid that he would insist on heading up to The Parkway and giving Moran a piece of his mind. As much as I would have enjoyed seeing Moran getting chewed out by my father, for Dad's safety I needed to calm him down.

"I'm sure he does. Maybe he just wants to make sure. I mean, he had seven of his guys gunned down."

"Yeah, yeah." Dad seemed to relax a bit. "That's not how you got that shiner, I hope. Trying to convince Moran you were telling the truth?"

"No, Dad, I didn't get this from Moran or his goons." Dad seemed convinced, and he should have been. I was telling the truth.

"Dinner's ready," Sarah yelled from the kitchen.

"I told you to go tell them, not yell it. Now every *nebish* and *chiam yankel* in the neighborhood will be coming to dinner," Mom chided Sarah loud enough for everybody else in the neighborhood to hear her too.

I got up and headed to the dining room with Dad as Sarah and Mom continued to argue. Dad took Mom's side of the argument as soon as he entered the dining room. *It sure is nice be home for a home-cooked meal.*

Chapter 16

Dinner was excellent—it was way better than anything that I could ever have come up with on my own. Sometimes I wonder why I ever left home. Of course, the constant yelling between Mom, Dad, and Sarah was a good reminder of why I had left. They—and I—had argued about all sorts of things, from what was going on in the neighborhood, to ward politics, to why I hadn't been at Temple in over a month. This was all well and good, as most of the time my folks' attention was on other things, or my sister, both of which suited me just fine. Sarah didn't like this attention, so she took a jab at my new girlfriend, and that triggered Mom into giving me the "third degree" about my love life.

Apparently, Mrs. Rabinowitz had told Mom everything that she knew about Moira. Granted, that wasn't much, but it was enough to set Mom on the scent. I spent the last half of dinner trying to fend off her probes and attacks, while Sarah just sat there and smirked at me. Honestly, I would have rather gone back and dealt with Mr. Brown.

I managed to escape by explaining that I needed to get some rest before going in to work. Working a night job does have some advantages, and I hadn't told a lie to my parents. I should have headed home and gotten some sleep before heading to work, but instead I was now walking north along Broadway, having gotten off the L at Wilson station. It was after eight p.m., it was bitterly cold, and I was really tired. I really *should* have gone home after dinner and gotten some rest, but I was still driven with the need to find Moira. I had to find her in order to make my plan work, and that was the only way that I could help protect my family.

I walked with my hands in my pockets, my collar pulled up, and my hat pulled down as far as it would go. It didn't help. A bitter wind was blowing in from off the lake and seemed to cut through me like a knife. I watched taxis and busses head up and down the street, carrying all sorts of people. Ladies in furs and men in evening dress walked out of fancy restaurants and probably more than a couple of speakeasies.

I paused and turned my back to the wind to light up a cigarette. I continued on, finishing my smoke as I approached the door to the Green Mill. Moira and I had come here the first night after we'd met in the diner, so as I walked toward the club, I half expected to see her saunter around the corner leading to the club door like she did that night.

It had been almost as cold as it was tonight, and she had turned the corner wearing a black flapper dress, fringed with red beads and she was wearing a long string of white pearls. She wore a red cloche hat with a mother-of-pearl cameo of a rose set in it. A lit cigarette had been nestled delicately in her left hand. She leaped into my arms, wrapping herself around me. I was unprepared and almost lost my balance as I tried to hold on to her.

She gave me a peck on the cheek, then jumped down

and grabbed my hand. "Come on, Saul."

"Aren't you cold?" I asked. I was bundled up and I was freezing.

"Don't be such a wet blanket." She pulled me forward and knocked on the door. A narrow window slid open and a rough, Italian-accented male voice said, "Wha'dya want?"

"Hey, Vinnie," Moira said.

"Moira," Vinnie sighed. "You know the rules. Ya gots to tell me the password."

"Oh, come on, Vinnie," she pouted, but Vinnie didn't budge. "Fine. Pineapples."

The window slid closed and Vinnie unlatched the door.

Now I stood outside the door to the speakeasy again. Nobody came to jump into my arms. Considering that a burly guy in worker's overalls came around the corner right then, I was pretty happy about that.

I walked down the narrow, brick-lined corridor and up to the thick wooden door. I knocked. The window slid open. I could see a pair of dark eyes look out at me. I could smell cigar smoke and cheap booze. "Wha'dya want?" I thought I recognized Vinnie's rough Italian voice.

"Pineapples," I said.

"Hmph." The window slid closed and the door opened. I couldn't tell if Vinnie was annoyed that I was able to gain access, or if he was just bored. I nodded to Vinnie as I walked through the door, but he ignored me.

The interior by the door was dark, but I knew my way, and after a few steps I walked through a dark curtain into the saloon. The room was brightly lit and I could hear a jazz band tuning up. Joe Lewis had sung jazz here until a couple of years back. The rumor around town was that Lewis had tried to leave the club to sing at another joint. A few days later, Lewis was found in his hotel room with his tongue cut out. Moira told me on our first visit here that she knew that the Green Mill's owner, Jack McGurn, had planned the attack on Lewis, not that the cops could ever pin anything on him. She had also hinted that Lewis' tongue hadn't been cut off using a knife but instead had been bitten off. She had laughed when she said it, so I wasn't sure if she was joking with me or not.

I walked past an empty booth near the middle of the bar. Moira had said it was Capone's reserved booth where he could sit and enjoy the music and still be able keep an eye on both the front and the back doors. It was always kept open in case Capone came in, even when he was out of state like he was now. I had been impressed on that first date that Moira was so well connected. She seemed to know everybody in the place, and everybody seemed to know her. At the time, I was happy just to bask in her glow—we'd gotten our drinks for free—but I'll admit that I was also a little jealous. I hoped now that Moira's popularity would work in my favor and that somebody would know how to find her.

I walked around the bar, my eyes scanning the crowd for any sign of Moira. The place was pretty crowded and noisy. The jazz band had started their set and was jamming away on the small stage at the back with a good crowd watching them play. The sounds of bass, sax, and trumpet rolled through the air and filled me with memories of Moira and me watching a band play here last week.

I shook my head; I couldn't continue dwelling on the past. I needed to find Moira today. I turned away from the band and surveyed the bar again. A couple walked away from the bar with their drinks and that's when I saw her. She was standing at the bar with her back to me, watching the band, her left hand holding a cigarette aloft as the fingers of her right hand twirled around the rim of her glass. She was wearing a blue jacket and was talking to a guy in glasses. I had a quick flash of jealousy, but shook it off. Hell, she'd flirted with practically everybody in the club the last time we'd come here. Why would now be any different?

I walked up and put my hand on her shoulder. "Moira, I've been looking everywhere for you."

She turned to look at me. Out of the corner of my eye I could see that the man she'd been talking to was turning red in the face. That should have been my first clue. I looked again and realized that this was not Moira, although she looked a lot like her, especially from the back. She had the same cut of hair, but her face was not as pale and her brown—not green—eyes were looking at me like I was some sort of slug. I quickly pulled my hand off her shoulder. "Uh, sorry...I'm sorry," I stammered. "You looked like somebody I know. Sorry."

I stepped back and turned away, coming face-to-face with Jack McGurn, who was laughing loud and hard. "You sure are some kind of suave son of a bitch."

I could feel my face reddening rapidly. I tried to laugh at myself, but it came out more like a strangled choke. I managed to say, "Give me a yak yak."

McGurn was still laughing when he grabbed a glass and a bottle. Even though he was a part owner of the place—some people said that he ran it for Capone—

McGurn liked to tend bar. McGurn set the glass down and poured me a couple of fingers worth of the drink. Yak Yak was an ugly 'bourbon' that was really just pure grain alcohol mixed with burnt sugar and iodine. I know, it sounds pretty bad but to be honest, the taste sort of grew on you. "Have you seen Moira?" I asked.

McGurn looked at me like I was drunk. "Who?"

I was a bit stunned. I'd spent a long night in this place with Moira, sitting at the bar as she held court with everybody around us, and as McGurn poured her glass after glass of gin that she never paid for. "You know, Moira. Moira Kelly. I was in here with her last week. Short red hair, green eyes, kinda pale skin."

Jack nodded. "Sounds like a lovely doll, but I don't remember her."

"How can you not remember her?" I pleaded. "You were giving her drink after drink on the house the last time we were in here."

"Now I know you're full of shit." McGurn laughed again. "Good lookin' dame or not, I don't give away drinks." To emphasize his point he held out his hand and I dropped a quarter into it. McGurn turned away.

I took a sip of the yak yak, my mouth grimacing at the taste. Yeah, I know I said that the taste grew on you. I didn't say that it was a good taste though. Fungus can grow on you, too.

I swirled the brownish liquid around in my glass wondering what I was going to do next. The band continued to play, starting a riff that proceeded for several chords before the saxophonist started in on a solo. I needed to find Moira, and the one place that I felt would be a sure bet to finding her was turning out to be a dead end.

I didn't have a clue as to where to look next, but I couldn't continue the search tonight. I needed to get to work. I couldn't afford to lose my job. There was no telling how Moran would react to me not being able to be his errand boy after all of his effort to make the offer.

I gulped down the last of the yak yak, my face contorting at the taste. I think McGurn, or whoever mixed this stuff up, had put a bit too much iodine in this batch. As I sat the empty glass down on the bar, the sound of an explosion came from behind me. I jumped and my hand slipped, causing the glass to slide across and off the back side of the bar. There were several screams and yells coming from around the speakeasy and the band had stopped playing. I turned around toward the noise along with everybody else in the joint.

Standing in the doorway stood a tall, plainclothes detective holding a shotgun, smoke lazily rising from the end of the barrel. Two uniformed cops stood just behind him, also holding shotguns at the ready. The detective yelled, "Nobody move! This is a raid!"

Oh shit, I thought. *Just what I didn't need.*

I glanced around the bar. People were panicking, a few ladies were still screaming, and everybody seemed to be doing the exact opposite of what the cop had ordered. People were running around, trying to get out of the place through both the front and back doors, which was hard since the cops were standing in the front doorway and I could see a couple more blocking the back door. I turned to look at McGurn, figuring that I'd take my lead from him. I hadn't heard of a raid on a speakeasy in a long time, certainly not since Mayor Dever had been in office. Sure, the distilleries and deliveries got hit a lot, usually by rival gangs, and sometimes Capone or

Moran would let the cops make a big bust to look good for the papers. I figured that this was a case of the cops flexing their muscle, or maybe making a point about a missed payoff or something.

I caught McGurn's eye just as he was ducking under the counter. He gave me a smirk, as if saying "better you than me", then disappeared. I gaped for a moment. *Where had he gone?* Then I remembered something Moira had said when we had first come to the Green Mill.

"That booth there," she said, pointing at an empty booth with her bright red, manicured finger, "is reserved for Al Capone. It's kept empty in case he ever shows up."

"Wow," I said. "Even when they know he's out of town?"

"You bet, sweetie. It's better to be prepared and keep Al happy all the time."

"But what if the place gets raided when he's here?" I asked. "I'm sure Capone wouldn't want to get caught in a raid."

Moira looked at me, her green eyes flashing as she smiled. "Smart boy. I knew I liked you." She pointed toward the bar. "There's an escape tunnel under the bar that leads out of here."

"Escape tunnel?" I gave Moira a curious look. "How do you know that?" She looked at me like I was an idiot. "I mean, sure, I guess most of these places have secret ways in and out. I just mean, how do you know that it's there behind the bar? I don't think that's the kind of info Capone would spread around."

She smiled and patted my knee. "I have my ways, dear."

Now, with people panicking and the cops rounding up everybody, I knew that the escape tunnel was my only way out. I shot a quick look around to make sure that the cops weren't close, then vaulted over the bar. I landed on my glass and almost fell, but recovered. I looked around, but I didn't see a door or anything at first. I crouch-walked to the spot where I had last seen McGurn.

"Where's McGurn? That lousy Irish prick." The detective's deep voice bellowed from the other side of the bar. "He's got a lot to answer for, that son of a bitch."

Looking around I could see a small button on the bar near the floor. I reached out and pushed it. There was a click, then the floor opened up right under me and I fell several feet.

"Ooof!" I landed hard. The fall knocked the wind out of me, but I couldn't just lie here. Chances were that somebody else might know about this tunnel and point it out to that bellowing detective in order to save their own skin. Grunting with effort I pushed myself up, trying to take shallow breaths. The trapdoor was still swinging above me and I banged my forehead into it.

"*Shtup!*" I swore, pushing the door up until I heard it click into place.

Rubbing my head, I looked around as I caught my breath. There was a small passage leading away from me, dimly lit by bare bulbs spaced widely apart. I headed down the passage. It was narrow in places and I bumped my shoulders a couple of times, but after a couple of minutes I came to a set of steps leading up. They creaked under me as I climbed, coming to a door, which opened when I gave it a shove.

I emerged into an alley across the street from the

Green Mill. I could see a couple of cars idling out front and people milling about. I pulled up my collar and straightened my hat as I headed up the alley, trying to look casual and not attract notice from the cops. Luckily, they were all focused on the Green Mill and weren't looking in my direction.

As I headed out of the alley and turned up the street, a body loomed out of the shadows and blocked my path. It took me a moment in the dim light to recognize the face of Agent Truesdale. Just as I did, I felt a rock hard punch to my gut, knocking the wind out of me for the second time that night. I let out a loud gasp of air and doubled over.

"Where do you think you're going, Saul?" Truesdale asked. "You wouldn't happen to be sneaking out of that speakeasy over there, would ya?"

I don't know if Truesdale expected an answer or not, but I was in no condition to say anything, so I just grunted.

"I thought you were a law-abiding citizen, Saul. Sneaking out of a speakeasy during a raid isn't something that an innocent man would do." He turned his head, "What do you think led him down this horrible path of crime?"

"I think it was that she-devil."

I now saw the slim form of Agent Wright standing behind Truesdale. I should have expected him to be here as well. *She-devil? Is he talking about Moira?*

"Look," I said, trying to summon some courage and get my breath back. "I don't know what you are talking about." I tried to stand upright. Truesdale put his bear-like hand on my shoulder and gave it a slight squeeze. I winced in pain.

107

"Look, Saul, I don't want to have to give you another bruise to match that shiner I gave you earlier."

"I think you already did." I tried to pull free but Truesdale held tight.

Truesdale turned and jerked his thumb toward a car parked nearby. "Let's go for a ride."

Chapter 17

It started snowing as Agent Truesdale led me to their car. It was a beat-up black Buick Standard Six, with worn paint work, rust along the fenders, and a crack in the front windscreen. "Wow, you Feds sure get some nice stuff," I couldn't resist the jab. At least when I'd been picked up by Moran's men, they'd been civil and had a nice car to ride in. All I'd gotten from Agent Truesdale had been a swollen face, a punch in the gut, and now a ride in this rattletrap. "What, couldn't Hoover afford to give you guys a decent car?"

"No, he was too busy hiring morons like you to work in the Post Office," Truesdale replied, though there wasn't any real malice in the retort.

Agent Wright jumped ahead and got behind the wheel of the Buick. The engine started with a cough and a cloud of exhaust, which only reinforced my first impression.

"Get in, Saul," Truesdale said, opening the door and half shoving me into the back of the car.

"Look, Agent Truesdale," I started as he climbed in next to me and closed the door. Agent Wright pulled away from the curb, painfully grinding the gears as he shifted out of first. "I've been trying to find Moira all day. By the fact that she's not here, you can see that I've not had any luck."

"I can see that. But I don't know if you were really trying. A late start this morning, followed by lunch and a leisurely stroll up Michigan Avenue. Then breaking and entering at a crime scene—what were you doing there, Saul? Followed by dinner at mommy's place, then an illicit night cap before work." Truesdale shook his head. "Yeah, you were trying really hard."

Ok, I know my mom raised a smart boy, but I was tired. *How'd he know where I'd been all day?* "Fuck you," I said. Not really witty I know, but I had had enough of Agent Truesdale's bullshit.

Truesdale's right arm shot out and pinned my throat against the back seat. It hurt even more than it normally would as it was still bruised from my earlier encounter with Mr. Brown.

"Listen, kike," he hissed. His breathe smelled like rancid sauerkraut. "Don't get smart with me. We know everything that you did today. Now tell me where your girlfriend is. Why are you protecting her?"

"I'm...not..." It was a struggle to get the words out with Truesdale's arm crushing my throat. "...protecting...her." Truesdale finally released me, and I rubbed my throat. "Look," my voice was raspy. "The only times I ever saw Moira were at the diner, my place, or the Green Mill." I left out our trip up to North Clark on Valentine's Day; I don't know if it was by accident, or if my subconscious decided to do it on purpose. Either way I wasn't going to correct myself and give these two even more information. "Hell, we went to the Green Mill just last week, and they treated her like royalty. Free booze, everybody there falling over themselves to be seen with her." I glanced out the window at the falling snow. "When I went there tonight they'd never even heard of

Moira. It was like she never existed."

"That witch must have had them under one of her evil spells," Agent Wright said from the front. He ground down another gear as he pulled to a stop at a traffic light.

"What the fuck are you talking about?" I asked. I didn't like Moira being called names, but Agent Wright sounded like he was crazy or something.

"Your girlfriend is—" Agent Wright started to say something, but Truesdale cut him off with a cough, or maybe it was a growl.

"So your sayin' that you don't know where she lives?" Truesdale asked.

"No," I looked at him. "Although maybe I should ask you, since you seem to know everything."

"Oh, we know a lot of shit." Truesdale groused. "Knowing stuff about you has been child's play. It's been great training for Agent Wright, here, though it hasn't been very difficult. A troop of blind Boy Scouts could follow your ass around this city. But your girlfriend is an enigma." He stressed the E, drawing it out. "It's as if she can disappear at will. Nobody can ever seem to recall seeing her, even those people who have spent an entire evening with her. She's the fucking invisible woman."

I could almost sympathize with Agent Truesdale. Since I'd started dating Moira she'd always come to me for our dates. She'd always suggested where we went and what we did. I said, "Then why the fuck don't you believe me? I don't know where in the hell she is."

"Maybe you should try looking there," Agent Wright said under his breath, though I still heard it. I looked toward Agent Wright to ask him what he meant, but I was pushed back in the seat as he accelerated the car with a lurch.

"I do believe you, Saul" Truesdale said, actually sounding like he meant it. "I just want to make sure that you understand just how important finding your girl-friend is to us."

"But why?" I asked.

"You don't need to know why," Truesdale growled. "Just make sure that you find her. And when you do, we had better be the first ones that you call."

The car pulled to a stop with a stutter and cough. The engine died as Agent Wright forgot to put in the clutch. I glanced out and noticed that we had stopped outside the Post Office.

"We need you to help us," Agent Wright said from the front. "And we are trying to help you."

I opened the car door and got out. "You could have fooled me."

Chapter 18

I don't really recall what happened at work that night. I'm sure that I sorted some mail—that was my job, after all. I think Joe was his usual self. He tried to tell me that he and Francine had gone out Saturday night. Since I had run into Francine at the diner Sunday morning and she hadn't said anything, I figured that he was lying. I really didn't care though, so I didn't call Joe out on his fantasy life.

I spent almost the entire shift brooding over my failure to find Moira. I couldn't protect myself or my parents if I couldn't find her.

I blew off Joe after our shift. I wasn't in the mood to watch his feeble attempts to try to woo Francine. If Joe was upset that I was running off again, I didn't care. I headed out into the cold morning, fresh snow covering the ground. I'm sure that to some people it looked pretty. It just made my feet cold.

I walked to the L station and climbed up to the platform where I caught the train. As I rode the L, I watched the city pass by—city buses, taxies, and people heading to work this Monday morning were quickly turning the snow to grey mush. The sky was a thick overcast, the grey clouds fitting my mood. It was a depressing start to the work week.

I got off the L and walked up the street to my apartment. I should have stopped at the bakery for some bagels or something to eat, but I didn't really care if I ate or not. I trudged up the stairs, hoping that Mrs. Rabinowitz would not pick this morning to be nosy. I tiptoed past her door, and luck seemed to be on my side as her door stayed closed. I continued up to my apartment and unlocked the door.

"Hey, Saul."

I almost jumped out of my skin at her appearance in my apartment. Moira was sitting at my kitchen table, a mug of coffee in her hands. She was wearing brown pants and a light blue shirt with a white sweater. A blue hat sat on the table. I finally recovered from my shock and shut the door.

"Where the fuck have you been?" I asked. I took off my coat and sat down at the table.

"Watch your language, Saul. What would your mother say?"

I ignored her. "I've been looking all over town for you."

"That's sweet of you, Saul," Moira patted my hand. "But you don't need to go looking for me; I'll be there when you need me."

"But why did you leave Saturday morning? Where did you go?"

"I went out," she said. Her voice had a slight edge to it, but that wasn't going to stop me from getting some answers.

"Out where? Why did you leave?"

"I just had to go out, okay, Saul? Don't worry about it. It's none of your business."

Her voice had a definite edge to it now, so I dropped it. "But the Feds showed up. They told me that I had to find you and bring you to them. Why do the Feds want you?"

"I know they were here." She pulled out the note that I had crumpled up and tossed into the sink and flattened it out on the table. "They aren't important."

"Not important!" I practically yelled. "One of them gave me this," I pointed to the shiner I still had on my face. "And gut punched me last night as well. If I don't give you to them then my parents are dead and I'm dead because they have the books Moran wants."

"Wait," she held up a hand and glared at me with those pretty green eyes of hers. "You went to see Moran?"

"It's not like I had any choice in the matter," I said. "He sent two of his thugs to bring me to him Friday morning. He told me about some raid the cops made on Ralph Capone's place, and that they had found some books that showed Capone's finances. He also told me that Capone was going to try to use me to get the books. Moran told me to get the books for him, and my Dad told me some Northsider goons were sniffing around the packing plant asking about him."

Moira sat quietly for a minute. Finally, she said, "It still doesn't matter."

I was about to protest, but she gave me a look that stopped my comment in my throat.

"Put your coat back on, Saul. I need to take you to meet somebody."

"But what about the Feds? They've been watching me like a hawk. If they find out that I saw you and didn't tell them, they're gonna get pissed. Besides, if we go talk to them, maybe we can get this all sorted out. Everything will be fine."

"Forget about the Feds," Moira said as she stood up. "I told you they don't matter."

She seemed so unlike her normal self. She wasn't as outgoing as she normally was. It was like she was acting mechanically, like she'd been told to do something distasteful.

"But if we go see the Feds we can get this straightened out and my folks won't get killed by Moran." I continued to sit and stared up at Moira. I was being stubborn about this, but I was tired and I still felt that getting Moira to the Feds was the best option to get me out of this horrible situation.

"Look, Saul," Moira sighed. "I know that you think that you're doing the right thing, but you're not. We can't let the Feds get involved. Now get your coat on, sweetie." She leaned down and gave me a slow kiss.

As she pulled back, she gave me a sweet, almost sad smile and looked at me with wide eyes. I didn't want to make her upset, so I grabbed my coat and put it back on. I didn't understand how seeing the Feds was wrong, and I really wanted to call Agent Truesdale, but I guess that would have to wait. Maybe if I went with Moira now she'd agree to go with me to see Agent Truesdale later.

We walked downstairs and passed Mrs. Rabinowitz coming up the stairs carrying a basket with some bread and sausage in it. She was about to say something, but a glance from Moira shut her up before she could even speak. Seeing Mrs. R silenced was a first. I gave her a weak smile and a little wave as we passed.

Outside, we walked up the street to West Chicago Avenue. There, Moira hailed a cab, which pulled to a stop in the wet slush in front of us. Moira and I climbed into the back.

"Where to?" the cabbie asked.
"7244 South Prairie Avenue," Moira said.

Chapter 19

I wasn't sure why the cabbie's eyes widened when Moira gave him the address, but it must not have been all that important since he pulled the cab into traffic and headed south.

Turning to look at Moira, I asked, "Who are you taking me to see?"

"Not here," Moira replied. "I'll tell you when we get there."

"Why can't you tell me now?" I insisted. Yeah—it was starting to become a habit of mine. "We need to talk about how we'll handle the Feds."

"Shhh," Moira put her hand to my mouth to silence me. "I told you earlier they aren't important. Just sit still and be quiet."

I turned to face the front of the cab and shut up. I obviously wasn't going to get any answers from her while we were in the cab. We drove south and I watched the traffic and people heading to work, or wherever it was that people went at 9 o'clock in the morning.

I turned back to look at Moira. The gray light of the morning seemed to make her look even more pale and ashen than normal, but she was still striking. Her face was sharp and angular with a slightly upturned nose. Her eyelashes were long and dark and complemented her dark green eyes. I know it sounds silly, but while I adored her and would do anything for her, I was conflicted between my desire to protect Moira from what was happening to me and my natural instinct to protect my parents.

I must have been staring at Moira for a couple of blocks. She finally noticed and stared back at me. Her gaze was penetrating, intimidating, and predatory. She looked like a cat about to pounce, although her gaze reminded me more of a snake in the way that she stared and didn't blink at all. A shiver ran up my spine and I went back to looking out of the cab's window. We were passing Washington Park, the ground covered under the fresh snow from last night and as yet unspoiled by any footprints.

I wanted to reach over and hold Moira's hand. Hell, I wanted her to reach over and hold my hand. I knew she'd never do the latter, and if I tried the former right now I was afraid that she'd bite it off. The cab hit a pothole and the bounce of the car shot a wave of pain through the wound in my stomach. I had hoped that it would have healed by now, but it was still lingering.

We turned a few more times and the cab pulled up to the curb and stopped. "Here ya go, lady," the cabby said.

I got out of the cab and looked around. It was a nice looking neighborhood. Most of the houses were single-story homes, with small lawns and a few trees that were covered in snow. Set between two of these small homes was a two-story red brick house. It had a wide set of steps on the right side of the house that led up to a porch and the front door. Above the front porch was an open balcony. Three tall bay windows were set in the wall to the left, a matching set on each story.

Moira got out and said something to the cabbie. The engine shut off, so she must have told him to wait. She crossed the street and headed up the walk to the house. The sidewalk had been shoveled, the snow neatly piled to the right of the walk. I hurried to follow her, calling out, "Okay, we're here. You can tell me your big secret now."

Climbing the stairs to the porch Moira ignored me and knocked twice on the door. It was quickly opened by a young man in a loose-fitting coat, white shirt, and tie. He nodded to Moira as if he knew her, but didn't say anything. He turned and led us through the entryway, down a narrow hall, and to a large wooden door. The house was nicely decorated and, although I'm no judge of art, I expected that the pieces hanging on the walls and the furniture that I could see were all worth a lot of money. I also saw a couple of other men in the house who were dressed like our unlikely butler. I was starting to get a little worried, *who's house is this?*

The man left us and headed back to the front of the house. I started to ask Moira what the hell was going on, but the words died in my throat as she gave me a stern glare. Moira waited a moment, and she took a deep breath before she knocked on the door. I heard a muffled voice say, "Come in" from the space beyond. Moira opened the door and she led me inside.

I stopped in my tracks and stared, and I'm sure that my mouth fell open. The man himself, Al Capone, was sitting behind a large desk.

"Please come in, Mr. Imbierowicz," Capone said.

Chapter 20

I don't know anybody who lives in Chicago that wouldn't recognize Al Capone. He sat behind a large mahogany desk, the morning papers laid out neatly on the desk top, a coffee cup sitting next to the papers. A green-shaded desk lamp cast a bright light across the headlines. A lit cigar sat smoking in a gold ashtray and a white, gold-trimmed telephone sat on the corner of the desk.

Capone sat with his fingers clasped, his hands resting on an ample belly. He was heavy-set, his round head resting on a short neck; it looked like his head was attached directly to his shoulders. He had dark brown hair, slicked back, with light grey eyes and shaggy eyebrows. His nose was somewhat flattened and he had wide lips. I could see that his face was whiter than normal, like he had applied talcum powder or something else to make it white. I couldn't believe somebody who'd just come from Florida could be so pale.

Capone made a gesture, and three henchmen rose from the sofa and chairs in the room and walked out. The last man closed the door behind him.

The room was now empty except for Capone, Moira, and me. Capone stood up from his chair. He was wearing a powder blue suit, with a white shirt, and blue silk tie. His tie was held in place with a marquise-cut diamond tiepin, and I could see a watch chain encrusted with diamonds stretching across his abdomen. He held out his hand, and as I shook it, I saw the largest diamond I had ever seen in my life. It probably cost more than I'll ever make in my lifetime.

"Welcome, Mr. Imbierowicz." His voice was soft and genteel, but I could hear the faintest echo of his Brooklyn roots. "Please have a seat." He gestured to two red leather chairs in front of the desk. Moira sat down instantly, but I hesitated. I don't know why; maybe I was stunned by being in the presence of the most famous—and probably also the most fearsome—gangster of Chicago, and maybe even the entire country. Maybe I was just dumb, but I couldn't get the newspaper article from the day after the massacre out of my mind. I had read that article through multiple times trying to find out any news about Moira. The paper had clearly said that Capone had been on vacation in Florida.

"Aren't you supposed to be in Florida?" I blurted out. Moira turned away, maybe in embarrassment. A look of irritation flashed in Capone's eyes, but it was quickly gone.

"I was in Florida," he said. "You might say I still am. I have over two dozen people down there who will swear to any cop, jury, or newspaper man in the country that I'm there right now. In fact, I would have preferred to stay in Florida, but the situation here in Chicago has gotten out of hand." Here Capone gave a meaningful glance to Moira. "I needed to come up here to make sure things got taken care of...personally."

He gestured for me to sit again, and this time I did. I glanced at Moira, my mind racing. Moira had hinted that she 'knew people' in town, and her actions at the Green

Mill had also suggested that she had connections. But until my last breath, I would never have guessed that she was connected to Al Capone.

"A few weeks ago," Capone said as he took his seat, "the cops made a raid up in North Chicago on a warehouse where some slot machines were being stored." Capone waved his hand in dismissal. "A feeble gesture by gnats. But this time the cops got lucky. They managed to get some financial books belonging to my brother Ralph. Instead of leaving what was clearly personal property alone, the cops decided to confiscate these books. The cops then turned these books over to the Feds. I have heard from reliable sources that the Feds hope to use these books to get my brother on not paying his taxes." Another dismissive wave.

"Can you believe the audacity of the Feds?" Capone asked. "Thinking they can get us to pay legal taxes on money made illegally! It's a joke, that tactic will never work on me, and I'll make sure it won't work on my brother either."

Capone looked at me, his light grey eyes giving me a penetrating gaze. "Now, if the cops had been sensible, they would have kept the books. I own this town from the cops to the mayor. I would have been willing to enrich their lives in exchange for the books, but they made a different choice.

"Now, I won't make a big fuss with the Feds. I don't want them to think they have something important that they can use, but I also don't want them to have the books either. I could easily make a move to take back what is, by rights, my property. But if I do that, if I get involved personally, or if any of my many associates get involved, then the Feds will become suspicious and they'll start to think that maybe this tax stuff is a good way to take down my organization. They will become even more of an annoyance than they are now."

Capone leaned back in his chair, resting his hands on his stomach. "But if the books should happen to end up missing, then the Feds won't have a case against Ralph and they won't have a new way to bother me or my family. But how to make the books disappear?" Capone shifted his gaze to Moira. I looked at her and saw that she seemed to sink into her chair. I was a bit stunned. I had never seen Moira cowed by anyone before.

"I had Moira here look for a suitable person who'd be able to get the books for me. Somebody who would have access and who could take the fall if they got caught."

What the hell? Realization hit me; Capone was going to use me as his patsy! I guess I shouldn't have been shocked, it's not like I was anybody important. The realization struck me hard because I immediately knew that Moira had been using me. I looked at Moira, but she was ignoring me. Capone's gaze was still locked on hers.

"Moira likes to work in her own special way," Capone continued. "She spotted you on her first day. A green mail sorter, desperate for a little love and attention. You fell for her so hard; she barely had to use any of her 'special' charms on you." Capone laughed, a couple of sharp sounds that were suddenly ended. "But then, just when she should have been making her move to get you to do this job, she goes and gets herself shot. Because of this, you are not yet aware of the important part that you will play in making my wishes come true because she fucked up. She fucked up so badly that I had to come back to Chicago to get this fuckin' mess straightened back out." Capone's voice rose slightly at the end, but he seemed to quickly regain his composure. He sat up and reached for the cigar on the desk.

"So now, Mr. Imbierowicz," Capone turned his gaze upon me, his eyes went cold and his voice dropped a bit, into a soft, polite tone. "You will get the books the Feds have and deliver them to me." Capone smiled as he puffed on the cigar.

I had been expecting Capone to ask me this since I had walked into the room. Even so, I was still a bit shocked by his demand, and I was a bit incensed at the way he had insinuated that Moira had failed him. *Like she got shot on purpose? Doesn't he understand the pain and suffering that she went through? And just how am I supposed to get these books for him?* As soon as I do, Moran will take out his revenge against my parents. It was a long-shot, but I needed to see if I could make Capone see reason. He obviously didn't know that Moran had already made basically the same offer to me. Maybe if he knew, he could relieve the pressure on my parents.

"No," I said.

"What!" Capone exploded into a rage. His face turned a deep crimson-purple color. "How dare you say no to me! Me! I own this fuckin' town, and no two-bit, low-life kike is going to tell me no!" His voice had gone from silky smooth to rough, back-alley hood in an instant. The words and his attention had been directed at me, but Capone quickly shifted his gaze to Moira. "How does a little shit like him dare to stand up to me?"

Capone turned his attention back to me, his face contorted by anger and rage. The blood had completely drained from his face, leaving it ashen. His eyes were wide and his nostrils flared. "You'll get me those god damn books, you fuckin' kike, or I'll chop your dad's head off, disembowel your mom, and throw your sister into the worst hell-hole of a brothel that I own, where she'll spread her legs for every lowlife in the state." He shoved the cigar across the desk and pointed it at me. "And then I'll string you up and bleed you dry." He stood up from the chair. He seemed to tower over me, or maybe I had shrunk down into my own chair. Fear curdled my stomach, not only for my own safety, but also for that of my parents and sister. It was my fault that now I had the two biggest gangsters in Chicago using my family as leverage against me. I was in a corner, and my only option, to use Moira to help me with the Feds to get the books for Moran, had just gone up in a puff of smoke when Capone had exploded.

"Okay, yes, yes," I stammered, holding out my hands defensively in front of me. Capone was leaning so far over his desk, I half expected him to leap on me and tear my throat out right there. Even though that wouldn't have helped his cause in the slightest, I still had that impression. "I know where the Feds are keeping the books, and I can get them for you in a few days, once I figure out how to get into the room."

Capone seemed to immediately relax, as if somebody had thrown an electric switch. He smoothed down his suit coat and tie. He passed a hand through his hair, even though it had stayed perfect throughout his tirade. "That's good to hear, Mr. Imbierowicz. Very good."

Capone sat back down and took another puff on the cigar. The bluish smoke rose up around his eyes, which I swear seemed to have been cast in shadow. It must have been a trick of the light. "I apologize for my outburst. I'm a man who is accustomed to getting what he wants."

"No, Mr. Capone," I said. I felt that I needed to settle

things down, to reassure Capone that I wanted to help, but that things were tricky. "I'm the one who should apologize." This seemed to have had the desired effect, as I could see Capone relax.

"I should have explained myself better," I continued. "I would like to get the books from the Feds for you, but I'm in a real bind. You see, Mr. Moran has already asked me to get the books for him, and…"

Capone's face reddened again, but he seemed to be able to control his anger better this time. He did give Moira another long, meaningful look.

"And, well," I continued. "Mr. Moran has also threatened the welfare of my parents if I don't get the books for him. I hope you can understand my predicament."

Capone gave me a slight smile. "Certainly. I am a family man myself and I adore my wife and children. I can understand your desire to protect your family from the likes of Bugs Moran."

I nodded. Even though Capone had also just threatened my family, I thought it best to not make that comparison.

"That is certainly a new development that I had not foreseen." Again, Capone gave Moira a look that seemed to say that she'd failed him. "I will take that information into consideration. But you need to remember what is important here, Mr. Imbierowicz. You need to get me those books from the Feds," he leaned across the desk, cigar clinched in his right hand as he braced it against the edge of the desk. Now his eyes really did seem to be cast in shadow, and took on a red glint—*another play of the light?* "Or all those things that you think Moran could do to your family will pale in comparison to what I will do to them if you don't."

I nodded dumbly. People like Capone and Moran got to where they are today by making, and following through on, threats like this. It was pointless to think that, once I'd gotten into their sights, that I or my family would ever be safe.

Capone gave a slight nod in acknowledgement at my grasp of the situation. He stood up, put the cigar in the ashtray, and walked to the door. "Moira, dear," he said, grabbing the door handle. "Please take Mr. Imbierowicz home."

Moira nodded and stood up. She'd not said a word since we'd entered the house, and I was starting to wonder what had gotten into her.

Capone smiled, but it was not a pleasant smile. It was more like the smile that a tiger might give to its prey when inviting it home for dinner. "Then come straight back here. You and I need to talk."

Chapter 21

The cab was still waiting for us when we left Capone's home. The driver started the engine and took off as soon as we closed the door; apparently the driver knew where to go, even though nobody had said anything. I started to ask Moira if Capone was always that excitable but I thought better of it. The only Capone I knew was the one that I read about in the papers: the guy who gave out presents to local kids at Christmas, the guy who provided meals to folks at Thanksgiving, the guy who generally helped out those in need. Everybody in Chicago knew that Capone was a mobster, but he was *our* mobster and we liked him. Moira just stared out the car window, her eyes apparently not focused on anything. I could tell that her thoughts were somewhere else.

I turned my own gaze out the window and watched the city as we drove along. Last night's snow had turned to grey mush on all the roads, giving the city a dreary appearance. As we passed the stockyards, I realized that I had just promised to deliver something that I didn't have to a second person who had both the ability and the willingness to kill me and my entire family. Oh, don't get me wrong—I knew Moran had the same ability— but after meeting Capone in person, and experiencing his anger first hand, I feared him more.

Suddenly, I felt Moira's lips brush my cheek. It startled me and I nearly bumped my head against the cold car window.

"Don't be so jumpy," she giggled. Like Capone, she was able to turn her emotions on and off at will. I stared at her. She stared back at me with her deep green eyes. "Everything will work out."

"Yeah, I know," I said. Somehow I felt better. I knew that Moira would make everything alright. The realization that she had been using me for Capone from the beginning was a forgotten memory. All that mattered was that she was back, and together we'd figure out how to get out of this mess. "It just seems like an impossible task."

"And I have complete faith that you can accomplish the impossible if you just put your mind to it." Yeah, it sounded really corny, like something from a Hallmark card, but coming from Moira it sounded like the divine wisdom being handed down to Moses from on high. She leaned over and kissed me, giving my lips a little nibble as she pulled back. I breathed a sigh of relief.

The cab pulled up outside my tenement. It had started to snow again, the fresh snow covering up the grey slush from this morning. I opened the car door and let Moira out. I started to pay the cabbie, and Moira leaned down and said, "Don't worry, it's been taken care of." I gave her a look, then shrugged and got out of the cab. The cab pulled away as we turned and headed inside.

It wasn't much warmer inside as we climbed the stairs to my apartment. Uncharacteristically we passed Mrs. Rabinowitz's door without any interruption from her and headed up to my floor. As we reached the landing Moira stopped cold, her hand grabbing my arm in a painful grip.

"Ouch," I yelped.

"Somebody is inside your apartment," She whispered. I felt her body tense, her stance changing slightly. She reminded me of a cat about to pounce on a mouse.

"Well of course there is. Everybody and their uncle has been in my apartment lately, so what else is new?" I reached for the door knob. "Let's see who it is this time. Two bits says it's my mom."

The door was unlocked and I opened it to see three men in my kitchen. *Apparently, I was wrong.* Bugs Moran was sitting in my favorite chair. *Why does everybody pick that chair to sit in?* Behind him, looming in the small kitchen space, stood Cup and Glass who had taken me to see Moran the first time. Glass glared at me from under his cheap fedora, and Cup gave me a slight nod as he pulled a toothpick from between his teeth.

I sighed, shrugging off my coat and placing it on the back of the empty chair. "Mr. Moran, what a pleasure to see you again." I didn't hide the sarcasm in my voice.

"I have been informed, Mr. Imbierowicz, that not only is the Beast back from his trip to Florida, but also that you have been to see him personally."

I started to reply but Moira cut me off. "No. Mr. Capone is still in Florida." Her voice was silky and smooth. I seemed to recall that she'd used the same voice when we'd gone out to dinner and for drinks.

Moran appeared to ponder this, then said, "My mistake. I must have been misinformed." He gave a dirty glance to Cup who shrank back a bit. Turning back to us, he continued, "Either way, I can't let Capone get his hands on those books. When are you going to get them away from the Feds for me, Saul?"

"Look, I know where the Feds are keeping..." I couldn't finish my sentence as Moira cut me off again.

"Look, Moran," she said, focusing Moran's attention on her. Her voice was still smooth, but there was an edge to it now, almost a deep growl that underscored her words. "Saul will get the books for you, but you're going to need to give him more time to get them away from the Feds." She gave Moran a long, hard look. I swear that Moran actually flinched before he turned back to look at me.

"Fine," he spat the word out. "You've got two days, Mr. Imbierowicz, but that's it."

"Then you'll have the books and you can use them to get Capone out of the picture, just like we agreed," Moira said.

Moran gave her a glance and nodded his head. "But after the fiasco last Thursday, you've not completed your part of the deal, my dear. You still owe me—"

Moira cut him off. *Hey, at least it wasn't just me she was rude to.* "I know, and I'm working on it. But we can't discuss it here."

I looked between Moran and Moira, confused. *What the hell is going on here?*

"Moira," I started to say, but she put her finger to my mouth and the words died on my lips.

Moran stood up and gestured to Cup and Glass. They started to leave the apartment, but Moran paused in the doorway. "Two days, Mr. Imbierowicz," he said, holding up two pudgy fingers. "Then I expect to have those books." He turned, and I could hear the three of them head down the stairs. Moira closed the door behind them.

"What the hell is going on?" I blurted out.

Moira gave me a gentle look, her green eyes seeming to fill my world. "It doesn't matter, Saul," she said. "Just make sure you figure out how to get the books away from the Feds. Let me handle the rest." She stroked her hand gently down the side of my cheek. I felt better knowing that all I needed to do was to figure out how to get the books away from the Feds and that Moira would handle the rest.

"Oh, and by the way, you owe me a quarter."

Chapter 22

Moira left a few minutes after Moran and his goons with my last quarter. It was almost one in the afternoon —*where had the time gone?*—so I was able to get a decent "night's" sleep before getting up at 8 o'clock to get ready for work. I slept like the dead, and felt refreshed when I woke up. I noticed that the bite on my stomach was still not healing, so I was a little worried about that. I made a mental note to pick up some iodine from the pharmacist as I cleaned the wound again. I didn't want it getting infected.

I actually had time to cook the hamburger that mom had brought over, and I was able to make a decent pot of coffee for once. I even managed to relax a bit as I ate my "breakfast". Finished with my meal, I put my dishes in the sink. Grabbing my coat, I headed out, being sure to lock the door—though, for the life of me, I don't know why.

It had stopped snowing, and it looked like the clouds had gone away as well, since I could see a couple of stars twinkling in the cold winter sky. I walked to the L, my breath freezing in the air as I whistled some jazz tune that I'd heard last week at the Green Mill with Moira. I felt refreshed and relieved. Sure, I still had to figure out how to get into that room where the Feds were camped out and steal the books, but that seemed like it would be a piece of cake now.

I got on the L and rode to the Post Office. I was a few minutes early and I managed to get clocked in and to my sorting station before Joe arrived. I was still whistling to myself when Joe came in and tossed his coat onto the rack in our sorting room.

"Why are you so damned chipper?" he asked.

"I finally got a decent amount of sleep today, for a change, and I even got to see Moira." *Oh, shit.* I regretted the words as soon as I said them, since Joe immediately started pestering me with questions. *Me and my big mouth.* I had to think quickly, and I spent the next hour explaining to Joe how Moira had come back to me, feeling sorry that she had run out, and that she had lied to me about seeing her sick aunt. Joe was of the opinion that Moira was just too flaky and that I could do better. I asked how he and Francine were getting along, which got me off the hook for a little while.

A few hours later, Joe was discussing the prospects for a Blackhawks win in a couple of days. They were on a four game losing streak, on top of an already dismal season. "I don't know why Gardiner can't seem to stop the damn puck from getting in," Joe was whining. "Hell, my blind grandmother could tend goal better than him."

I picked up a stack of letters from the basket. I was about to retort that it wouldn't matter how well Gardiner did if the rest of the team would actually score some goals, but I was distracted as I saw Mr. Dickenson walk onto the sorting room floor, leading two men I had seen too much of lately; Agents Truesdale and Wright.

"Ah, *dreck*," I swore under my breath. I thought about trying to make a run for it, or maybe just hiding, but Mr. Dickenson was already pointing at me and Agent Truesdale was striding over.

I tried to focus on the task of sorting the letters in my hands, but I couldn't see any of the addresses. Suddenly, my palms were sweating and my mouth had gone dry. I don't know why I was feeling so nervous, other than the fact that each time I'd met with Agent Truesdale he had either left me unconscious or out of breath.

I could feel Agent Truesdale as he loomed behind me. Joe also noticed his presence and stopped his discourse on the Blackhawks. "Whadda you want?" Joe asked.

Agent Truesdale didn't say anything. He just stared at Joe until he went back to sorting his letters. Truesdale had an intimidating way of looking at people, almost as good as Moira and Capone. *I bet he could stare a statue into changing its pose.* He turned toward me, pulling out a wallet from his coat. "Agent Truesdale, with the Bureau of Investigations," he announced as he flashed his badge. I stared at him open-mouthed. I was wondering what was up, since he had to know that I knew who the hell he was; then it dawned on me that he was making a show so that everybody else in the room didn't know that fact. For as much rest as I had that day, I was really slow on the uptake. "We need to ask you a few questions, Mr. Imbierowicz. Please come with me."

I thought about asking him what was going on, but I didn't want Joe to get any more curious than he already was. I tossed the stack of letters that I had been holding back into the sorting bin. I gave Joe a shrug, as if to say "I haven't got a clue what this guy wants" and followed Agent Truesdale out of the sorting room.

Agent Wright fell in step behind us. I looked back at him, and he smiled politely, but didn't say anything. Agent Truesdale led us to the elevators, pushing the button for the sixth floor. When the doors opened, Agent Truesdale led the way down the hall and around the corner, stopping in front of the same janitor's closet that I had seen the two of them use before.

I couldn't resist a jab. "You Feds seem to be as cheap with your offices as you are with your cars."

Agent Truesdale paused in unlocking the door and sneered at me but didn't rise to the bait. He finished unlocking the door and walked in, pulling the cord on a bare bulb. The light flickered, then shone brightly to illuminate a small metal desk pushed against one wall, a filing cabinet, and several shelves holding cleaning supplies. There was one chair, next to the desk, which Agent Truesdale wedged himself into. I stood in the doorway and Agent Wright squeezed past me, closing the door behind him and then taking a seat on the edge of the desk.

"How the hell did you guys get all this stuff in here?" I asked. With the furniture, shelves, and the three of us, we were packed in like sardines.

Truesdale ignored my question, pulled out a cigar, and lit it. Agent Wright did say something, but not to answer my question. "We thought we had an agreement, Mr. Imbierowicz." He sounded so formal, so bureaucratic. "We thought you were going to help us out. Now you've put yourself in a really bad position."

"What do you mean?" The words were out of my mouth before I could stop myself. I knew what they meant—why hadn't I called them when Moira had shown up?

"Stuff that shit up your ass," Truesdale said around his cigar. "You know what Christian is talking about. You were with your dame today, there's no sense in denying

137

it. So why didn't you call us?"

I leaned my head back against the door and sighed. *Why can't anything go my way these days?* "Yeah, I saw Moira today. She was waiting for me at my place when I got off my shift. I wanted to call you, honestly, but Moira said she didn't want to talk to you two *putzes*. She hung around for part of the morning, then left." I kept it as short as I could and I didn't want them to know that we'd gone to see Al Capone, or that Bugs Moran had shown up. I should have known better than to keep something from these two.

"Who did you go see?" asked Agent Wright. He was leaning forward on the edge of the desk, eager to hear my answer. Apparently they'd been watching my place when we left to go visit Capone.

"Look," I said, avoiding the question. "I still don't know why you guys want to talk to Moira. Why is she so important?" I was beginning to think I knew why, but I wanted to hear it from these two.

"It should be enough for you to know that she is important to us," said Truesdale. "Who did she take you to meet?"

"No," I said. I was getting either really brave, or, as I could see the expression on Truesdale's face, really stupid. "I won't tell you until I know why you want her."

"Why are you protecting that hell-spawned bitch?" I was a bit stunned as the question came from Agent Wright. He had always seemed so clean-cut.

"Don't you call her that," I nearly shouted. "You don't know anything about her."

"No," Agent Wright stood up from the desk. The small confines of the closet meant that he was standing chest-to-chest with me. He poked a finger under my nose. "You're the one who doesn't know anything about her. She's been playing you for a fool since the first day you met her. You have no idea what you are dealing with." I had never seen Agent Wright so indignant.

A part of me seemed to remember my anger at learning that she'd been using me as Capone's pawn, but I was surprised that these two knew that. I was also a bit stunned by Agent Wright's vehemence. I expected this kind of attitude from Truesdale, but not from Wright. I gave a glance at Agent Truesdale, who seemed to be getting a laugh at my expense.

"Christian," he said, blowing out a cloud of blue-grey smoke. "Maybe you should explain to Saul just what it is that we are dealing with here."

Agent Wright relaxed a bit and looked at Truesdale. He seemed to consider it for a moment, then resignedly nodded his head. He sat back down on the desk, brushing down his pants as he sat.

"Mr. Imbierowicz, what do you know about vampires?"

Chapter 23

"Vampires!" I laughed. "You mean like Count Dracula?" I had read Bram Stoker's novel when I was in high school. I shook my head and continued to laugh. "Now I know you guys are crazy. You two actually think Moira is a vampire?"

Truesdale just sat there, staring at me, blowing smoke from his cigar.

Agent Wright said, "Yes, we do." He sounded serious.

"Oh, come on," I exclaimed. "I read Dracula in high school. Aren't vampires supposed to sleep during the day in coffins and are afraid of the light and stuff like that? Moira and I have been together plenty of times during the day and she's never been afraid of the sun."

"And just how much sun is there in Chicago during the winter?" Truesdale asked. He had a point, but I wasn't going to acknowledge it.

"Look, Mr. Imbierowicz—Saul," Agent Wright sounded sympathetic. "We know enough about vampires to know that not everything in the stories and legends are true. But you need to believe us, they *are* real, and they are a growing threat to us."

"What?" I let the incredulity fill my words. "Are they're going to overthrow the entire human race, or are we just worried about Chicago and the next city election?"

Agent Wright ignored my comment and opened a drawer in the desk, pulling out a well-worn and aged book. I could see the words 'Holy Bible, King James Version' printed in fading gold leaf on the spine. Agent Wright opened the book to a spot already bookmarked. He read aloud, "'There is a generation that curseth their father, and doth not bless their mother. There is a generation that are pure in their own eyes, and yet is not washed from their filthiness. There is a generation, O how lofty are their eyes! And their eyelids are lifted up. There is a generation, whose teeth are as swords, and their jaw teeth as knives, to devour the poor from the earth, and the needy from among men', Proverbs chapter 30, verses eleven to fourteen."

Agent Wright closed the book solemnly and looked at me, a smug smile on his face, like he'd just proven some grand theorem in school.

"So you have some writings in a holy book that could mean anything," I said. I smiled as Agent Wright bristled a bit. "There are tons of stories my Rabbi told us about Lilith or Estrie or other 'demons'," I held up both of my hands, my first two fingers twitching up and down, "who go around eating babies and drinking blood. Big deal."

"But don't you see?" exclaimed Agent Wright. "The fact that descriptions of these creatures appear in so many holy texts, and in legends around the world, means that they have to be true. How else do you explain how so many people separated around the world came up with legends of similar creatures? The lamia in Ancient Greece, the vetalas in India, or the jiangshi in China. These creatures have existed since the Creation. My research—and that of others—suggests that vampires and other demons are the unholy spawn of Adam and Lilith after Adam and Eve were expelled from the Garden of Eden."

I stared at Agent Wright, then looked at Truesdale. "Don't tell me you believe this bullshit?"

"Son," Truesdale pulled the cigar from his mouth. "I'm not sure I fully believe Christian's take on these creatures, but this is a free country and he can believe what he wants. What I do know I have seen with my own eyes. During the war, there were rumors that men from both sides who had deserted their posts had fled into no-man's land. They survived by attacking other men and drinking their blood and eating them. Since the war, I have seen men attack other men, biting their victims and drinking their blood. I've seen men who were shot and not fall dead, continuing to move as if nothing had happened."

He knocked some ash from the cigar and gave me a cold stare. "I've seen men move so fast that they seem to disappear from one spot and reappear in another. And I've even seen a scrawny stick of a man—somebody no bigger than Christian here—lift somebody twice his weight off the floor by one hand. So yeah, I believe in these creatures."

My thoughts immediately went to my encounter with Mr. Brown on Sunday. "And what, the Government has you hunting them down? Some kind of vampire hit squad? And you think Moira is one of these vampires. Are you going to kill her?"

"Eventually," said Agent Truesdale evenly. "But for now, we just want to talk with her. See, we know very little about vampires..."

"We know they must feed on human flesh and blood

to survive," interrupted Agent Wright. "They can control people with their minds and force them to do their bidding. My research also suggests that they can change forms and control animals. They are not afraid, or hurt by, sunlight, but they are fearful of holy relics and strong faith, and can be hurt by blessed objects. To kill them you have to either stab them through the heart with a wooden stake or cut off their head."

"What, no fear of garlic?" I asked with a sneer. Agent Wright just glared at me.

"Despite what Agent Wright just said," continued Truesdale, "we still know damn little about them. See, what we have learned has come from piecing together bits here and there from folks who have been interrogated or from documents we've managed to find. One of the things we have learned is that the vampires seem to be infiltrating the gangs across the country, using the chaos and violence with the bootlegging and gang wars to get positions of power within the gangs. That's something the government cannot allow.

"We think your girlfriend might be a vampire, and that she might have a connection with a gang." *Boy, was he right there. Moira seemed to have connections to two of the biggest gangs in Chicago!* "We need to talk to her to find out what she knows. We have learned that she was turned into a vampire by somebody of power, and we want to know who this person is."

"You think Al Capone is a vampire?" I blurted out. The thought was so funny on the face of it that I couldn't help myself. The two agents stared at me, then exchanged a glance with each other.

"Why would Al Capone be a vampire?" asked Agent Truesdale. His stare bored into me.

I tried to ignore him, but it was so unnerving that I finally said, "Well....I mean...." *Damn. I'd certainly put my foot in it there.* I sighed. "That's who Moira took me to see today. Al Capone."

"Wait," said Agent Wright. "Al Capone is in Florida. I read that in the papers. Are you saying he's here in Chicago?"

"Yes. Look, I didn't know Moira knew Capone or anything until today. Like I said, she was waiting for me at my apartment when I got off work. We took a cab down to Capone's house south of town."

"What did you guys talk about?" asked Agent Wright.

"Oh, the weather, how bad the Blackhawks are, you know, the usual." The two agents just looked at me blankly. "Fine. Capone wants me to steal some books you Feds have." The two Agents gave me another blank look. "I thought it was you two who had them, but if you are the Government's fearless vampire killers, then I guess it's some other Federal agency that has the books."

"What are you talkin' about, son?" Truesdale asked.

"Apparently there was a police raid a few weeks ago on some gambling joint run by Capone. During the raid, the cops found a set of books that can be linked to Ralph Capone. The cops took the books and gave them to the Feds. Everybody seems to think that they might have evidence in them that could link Al Capone to all sorts of stuff and he wants them back. He's threatened to kill my family if I don't get the books for him, and since he and Bugs Moran both want the books..."

"Wait, Bugs Moran also wants the books?" asked Agent Wright.

"Yeah. I met him last week right after the massacre and he told me to steal the books for him. He also threatened my family."

Agent Truesdale gave a low whistle. "Boy, you are screwed." He chuckled as I glared at him. He held up a hand in a placating gesture. "Look, kid, we can protect your family from both of those goons, but only if you promise to help us out. If you're right and Moira is working for Al Capone, that makes things *very* interesting. Agent Wright and I need to discuss some things." Agent Truesdale stood up.

I looked from him to Agent Wright, and my mind was reeling from everything they had told me. The thought crossed my mind from earlier in the day about Moira also working with Moran on something, but I figured that things were complicated enough, so I kept quiet. One thing was bothering me though, and I self-consciously rubbed the spot where Moira had bitten me. "Agent Wright, how is a vampire created?"

"The vampire has to feed on a person at the neck over a period of a couple of days and also has to share their blood with the victim. Then, the person is turned into one of those godless filth." He gave me a glance, his eyes obviously looking at my neck for bite marks. I relaxed a little bit.

Agent Truesdale moved to open the door, handing me a card with a phone number on it. "If anything happens, call us at this number. Thank you for your cooperation, Mr. Imbierowicz."

Chapter 24

After leaving the two Agents, I returned to the mail room in a bit of a daze. I finished the rest of my shift mechanically, not really seeing what I was doing. Joe tried to get me to spill the beans on what the Feds had wanted, but I refused to say anything. That pissed Joe off, and he was mad at me for the rest of the shift.

When we got off work, I didn't bother to get breakfast at the diner. Instead, I headed out into the cold morning air. Everything looked different to me now. I glanced at people heading to work and I kept wondering if any of them might be vampires. *How can you tell?* If what Agents Truesdale and Wright had said was true, that Moira was a vampire, then anybody could be one. Moira was just a normal girl. She was attractive and fun to be around. Nothing about her manner suggested that she was anything different—except for how she had bitten me when we were making love. Despite Agent Wright's reassurance I was still worried about that. He seemed to know a lot about vampires, but certainly he didn't know everything. What if he was wrong about how a vampire was made? What if I was already turning into one and didn't know it? My skin began to crawl as I thought about it. *Man, what would Mom say if she found out?* I heard Mom's voice in my head, "What, it's not good enough for you to be a good Jewish boy, you had to run off and become one of the living dead? What kind of son would do that to his mother?"

I climbed the steps to the L and waited for the morning train. I kept glancing around, sure that people were staring at me like I was growing fangs and was going to attack everybody there. I shuffled away from the people on the platform, found a quiet seat on the train when it arrived, and generally avoided everybody as the train jostled along the tracks to my stop.

The sun was shining weakly as I climbed the steps to my tenement. I saw Mrs. Rabinowitz checking her mail as I walked in. Had I kept quiet, she might not have noticed me, but my mother had raised me to be polite.

"Good morning, Mrs. R," I said in greeting.

She looked up from the mail box, a hand held to her chest. "Oh, goodness! You startled me, Saul. You are as quiet as the dead."

I flinched at her words but managed to smile, "I'm sorry, Mrs. R. I didn't mean to frighten you."

She waved a hand dismissively. "That's all right, dear. I must have been absorbed in my own thoughts." She pulled out her mail and closed the box. A few letters fell to the floor and I walked over to help pick them up.

"Why do we get so many ads in the mail?" she asked wearily. I noticed that over half of her letters were advertising fliers and letters.

"I don't know, Mrs. R," I said. That was a small lie; I knew it was really cheap for businesses to send out ads directly to people. Hell, most of the mail I sorted was direct mail fliers and stuff.

"Well, can't you do something about it? It's all just so much junk."

I handed the letters back to her. "I'm sorry, Mrs. R.,

I just sort the mail." I turned and started up the stairs.

"Did you ever get that second lock for your door?" Mrs. Rabinowitz called after me.

"Not yet, Mrs. R. I will today," I lied as I continued up the stairs. I didn't want to have yet another conversation about my door with Mrs. Rabinowitz. I walked up the steps to my apartment and tried to open the door, but it was firmly locked. I was surprised. I had gotten so used to coming home and finding somebody in my kitchen that I had sort of expected it to be open. I unlocked the door and went in, hanging my coat on the back of a chair. I pulled out Agent Truesdale's card and held it a moment, flicking its edge with one finger. I wondered if I should have told them more about what Moira and Moran had said to each other but, since I didn't really know what was going on, how could I make them understand? I shrugged and tossed the card onto the table. I was not hungry, so I didn't bother with fixing anything to eat—not that I had anything in the icebox anyway.

I got dressed for bed and got under the covers, but I couldn't sleep. My mind kept replaying all the times that I had been with Moira, trying to figure out if there had been any clues that might have suggested that either the Feds were right, or that they were just completely loony. I still wanted to believe the latter, and I kept trying to find any reason to explain that Moira was not a vampire. I finally managed to fall asleep with that conviction firmly in my mind.

Intense pain in my cheek woke me up from a deep, dreamless sleep. My eyes flew open and I saw Moira leering at me. She stood on the left side with her left knee resting on the bed. She had on a thin, green-colored blouse that accented her eyes, which were wide with anger.

"Why did you fuckin' do it?" Her right hand came crashing across my face, the force of the blow such that I rolled across the bed, tangled in the quilt. I stared up at her, my eyes wide with fear. There was something feral and predatory in the look she was giving me.

"Do...do what?" I stammered. She climbed fully onto the bed to hit me again and I scooted back, falling with a sharp THUD onto the floor, my legs still tangled in the quilt .

"You went to the damned, infernal Feds last night," she spat. "You told them that you and I had met with Capone." She jumped off the bed, landing with her legs straddling me. I scooted away from her, finally managing to get my legs untangled from the quilt. My heart was racing and sweat was pouring down my sides. She stood there, raising an accusing finger at me. *Had her nails gotten longer?*

"You told those two fucking Federal assholes that Capone asked you to get the books for him. And do you know what those two pricks did?"

My back hit the wall and I stood up as I shook my head. "What?" I managed to say.

"They went and arrested Ralph Capone. Dragged him from his bed this morning in front of his family."

"Look," I said, holding up my hands. "I didn't have a choice. They made me tell them what I had done and who I had gone to meet. I didn't know what they were going to do."

"Liar," Moira spat out the word. Her face seemed contorted, and I could see a sharp fang protruding from

149

her lip as she sneered at me.

"It's the fucking truth!" I yelled. "They said that they could protect my family, so what was I supposed to do?"

"You were supposed to keep your fucking kike mouth shut and do what I told you to do, you god damn piece of shit." She slashed out with her right arm. She had moved so quickly that I was caught by surprise. I felt sharp claws rake across my chest, blood instantly welling up and soaking my shirt.

I turned and ran for the kitchen. I hadn't taken more than a couple of steps when she tackled me and I hit the floor. Her claws gouged my back, then she rolled me over and grabbed my shirt, pulling me up and off the floor. "You were such a fucking waste of my time and energy. Now I have no choice but to do my Master's bidding and kill you. " She looked at me, her green eyes seeming to bore into my soul. She licked her tongue across her teeth, flicking over two large fangs.

"You had such promise, Saul." Her voice was softer now, though there was still an undertone of a growl. "You were going to be my ace in the hole, my ticket to freedom, but now I'm forced to destroy my own creation or be killed myself. Such a fucking waste."

She casually tossed me across the kitchen, like I was some rag doll. I landed hard on the table, falling onto my favorite chair, which broke under me. The table crashed onto its side. I could taste blood in my mouth. "Moira, you don't have to do this," I pleaded.

"Yes, Saul, I do," she looked at me with a mixture of anger and sadness. "I have no choice."

She took a step forward and I managed to surprise her as I kicked out with my leg, knocking her feet out from under her. She landed hard next to me and I immediately sat on her, punching her in the face. My mom and dad would be furious that I was hitting a woman—they had raised me better than that—but I had been in enough scrapes in the neighborhood growing up to know that I should never give the advantage to an opponent, even if it was a girl. Besides, with those fangs, claws, and strength, I didn't know if she could still be considered a woman right now anyway. Monster was more like it.

Suddenly I felt a sharp pain in my groin and I gasped, the sound and air being cut off as Moira grabbed my throat. I tried to pull her hand free, but she had me in a vise-like grip. She leaned close and flicked her tongue across my cheek, and it came back red with my blood. "I could almost consider this foreplay, Saul," she said, then bit me hard on my right shoulder.

Somehow I managed to scream through her grip on my throat. My vision was starting to grey and I couldn't catch my breath. I continued to claw feebly at her hand. She brought her face up, my blood ringing her mouth and a small trail of it running down her chin. She seductively stuck out her tongue and licked the blood from her lips. "I'm so disappointed in you, Saul. If you'd only listened to me, none of this would have had to happen. But here we are, and you know what they say, when life gives you lemons..."

She tossed me back down. I hit the already broken chair, which shattered into pieces. I greedily gulped air, trying to breathe. My hands fighting for purchase on the floor, now slick with my blood. My right hand hit one of the broken pieces of the chair; part of the chair leg broken as a thick stake. Agent Wright's words from last night came rushing back to me. *To kill them you have to either stab them through the heart with a wooden stake or cut off their head.*

Moira knelt down, her hands caressing my back, the sharp claws casually drawing blood. I grimaced in pain. "Shhh," she soothed, sounding almost sensual. "Don't struggle. Struggling will just make it worse for you."

She grasped my left shoulder and rolled me over. As I rolled, I grabbed the chair leg and shoved it with all my remaining strength at Moira. I must have caught her by surprise. The chair leg hit her just below her left breast, my will driving it hard through her ribs. Blood immediately flowed from the wound, soaking her green blouse and dripping down onto my hand. Her eyes went wide in shock, and a small gasp of air escaped from her mouth, along with some frothy blood. She fell back on her butt, her right hand grasping at the stake, while her left reached out pleadingly to me.

"Saul," she gasped. "Please, don't let me die." Her voice was soft and pleading. I almost felt sorry for her, and thought about trying to pull out the stake, but the past couple of minutes had been a rude, and very painful, awakening as to what kind of creature Moira really was. I wasn't about to give her a chance to come back and finish what she'd started. More blood bubbled from her mouth, and her right hand was slick as it tried to grip the stake.

"Please, Saul. I love you." She reached out with a blood-soaked hand toward me.

I looked at her, fear and adrenaline continuing to pump through my body. "I love you too," I managed to say, then pushed hard against the chair leg, driving it in deeper and causing Moira to fall backwards. "But I think we should see other people."

Chapter 25

I sat in the middle of my kitchen; blood seemed to cover everything. My body began to shake uncontrollably and I reached out to steady myself on the fallen table. I choked back bile and had to turn away from the sight of Moira. My eyes fell on the card that Agent Truesdale had given me. It must have fallen off of the table during the fight. It was sitting in a small puddle of blood, but I could still read the phone number. I needed somebody to help me, and there was no way that the regular cops would be able to do that.

I reached out and grabbed the card and managed to pull myself up. My head swam, and the room seemed to tilt wildly until I grabbed hold of the icebox. I took a couple of deep breaths and closed my eyes. I used to get really dizzy playing on the merry-go-round in the park as a kid. Each time I did, I would close my eyes and count to ten, and that made the dizziness stop. It worked again this time, too. When I opened my eyes, the room had stopped spinning. I had hoped that the blood and Moira's body would have also been gone, but no such luck.

I headed out of my apartment and managed to get down the stairs without anybody—especially Mrs. Rabinowitz—seeing me. The last thing I needed was to try and explain why I was covered in blood to Mrs. R.

The tenement had one phone in a small booth in the entry hall. It was damned inconvenient to always have to come downstairs to make a phone call, but what do you expect for five dollars a week?

I dialed the number on the card. The phone rang once before it was picked up. "Agent Truesdale speaking," said a familiar, gruff voice.

"It's Saul," I croaked. "Moira and I just had a fight and she just tried to kill me. You need to get over here, fast."

"She tried to kill you?" Truesdale's voice asked.

"Yeah," I replied. "Otherwise I wouldn't be talking to you. But she won't be trying again either. She's dead."

There was silence for a few seconds, then Truesdale said, "Fine. We'll be over there right away. Don't go anywhere." He hung up.

I looked at the receiver, "And where the fuck would I go?" I asked as I hung up the phone.

I headed back up the stairs. Just then, Mrs. Rabinowitz came out of her apartment. *Damn!* She turned to greet me and gave a shout. "Saul, dear God, what happened to you?"

"I cut myself shaving," I lied. I tried to move past her, but she grabbed me by the shoulders. I grimaced as pain shot through my right shoulder where Moira had bitten me.

"Saul, you need to go to a hospital. What will your mother say?"

I rolled my eyes. Last thing I wanted was to tell my mother. "Look, Mrs. R., I just got off the phone with the police. They are sending people over and an ambulance. I'm fine, really."

"Why did you call the police? Did you have a burglar? You know I told you to get a second lock on your door."

"Yes, you've told me a million times," I said in irritation. "Look, I'm going to be fine. I just need to get upstairs and wait for the police."

She let me go and stepped aside so I could head up to my apartment. I could see a look of determination in her eyes. "And please," I said, giving her my best sad-eyed look. "Please don't tell my mother. I will let her know everything as soon as I can. If you say anything, you'll just scare her needlessly." Mrs. Rabinowitz seemed to ponder this, then gave me a small nod. I smiled, then headed upstairs to wait for Agents Truesdale and Wright to arrive.

The two Agents arrived about 15 minutes later. I was sitting in my living room with the lights off, shaking uncontrollably. The sun was just setting and I was trying to avoid the harsh sight in the kitchen. Agent Truesdale was the first through the door. He paused in the entryway, and I could hear a muttered, "Jesus H. Christ" come from him. He stepped around the blood and walked into the living room. I stood up on wobbly legs and could see Agent Wright standing in the doorway, crossing himself and glaring at Truesdale.

"You know, Saul," said Truesdale. "We wanted her alive so that we could ask her questions."

"Fuck you," I said, stepping into the light of the kitchen. Truesdale gave me a raised eyebrow as he looked at my wounds.

He pointed at me. "How much of that blood is yours, and how much is hers?"

I looked down at my wounds and shrugged. "About fifty-fifty, I'd guess."

Two men wearing orderly uniforms walked in carrying a stretcher. They didn't seem to show any reaction as they looked at the body. Apparently death was so commonplace in Chicago these days that nothing seemed to bother them, even a beautiful dame with a wooden chair leg through her chest. The orderlies opened the stretcher and picked up Moira's body, placing it on the stretcher. She looked so strange lying there, covered in blood with a chair leg sticking up out of her chest.

"What are you going to do with her?" I asked.

"We'll take her to the morgue, for now. Then we'll make arrangements to ship the body to Washington so the guys in lab coats can study her," Agent Truesdale grunted. "We need to get you looked at. That wound on your shoulder looks pretty bad."

I simply nodded; I guess I was in shock. But my shoulder was throbbing so I wasn't going to disagree with Truesdale. One of the orderlies pulled the chair leg out from Moira's chest, then covered her face with a blanket. They lifted the stretcher and Agent Truesdale said, "Let's get you out of here."

Chapter 26

"Ouch!" I winced as the nurse applied iodine to one of the wounds on my chest. She just shook her head at me but didn't say anything. My right shoulder now sported several stitches and had been covered by a large bandage. My back still stung from similar ministrations that the nurse had performed earlier. Agents Truesdale and Wright had taken me to Cook County Hospital for medical treatment and I was sitting in a hospital bed in a private room. Agent Truesdale had used his authority to insist that I be kept away from other patients. I looked at Agent Wright, who was standing just inside the door watching the nurse tend to my wounds.

"I need to get to work," I said.

"You won't be going to work tonight," Wright said. "Not in your condition. You just survived a serious assault. You need to rest."

"If I don't go to work I'll be fired," I protested. "And if I get fired I can't get the books and then my family is dead."

"We'll take care of that," Wright said. "We need you to stay put for our plan to work."

"Plan? What plan?" I stared at Agent Wright. He flushed a bit, so I knew that he had said more than he should have. I winced again as the nurse swabbed another laceration on my chest. With the nurse still here

I figured he wouldn't say anything, so I decided to not press him. "Never mind," I said. "As long as there actually is a plan."

Wright looked relieved. "Agent Truesdale is going to talk to your supervisor. You won't have any problems at work."

The nurse finished applying the last bandage to my chest. As she cleaned up her materials, a doctor entered the room. He wore a starched white lab coat and was smoking a cigarette. He walked over to my bed without acknowledging either Agent Wright or the nurse and grabbed my wrist to check my pulse. Apparently he was satisfied that I was still alive, because he then roughly pulled off the bandage on my shoulder.

"Aaaa!" I nearly screamed.

My complaint went unnoticed as the doctor probed my wound. I wanted to punch him for the pain he was causing me, even though I suppose that he was just doing his job, but he could have been a bit gentler with his touch. He grunted and was apparently satisfied as he reapplied my bandage. He then pulled down my hospital gown and checked the bandage that they'd applied to my stomach wound. Thankfully he pulled this one off more gently than the one on my shoulder. He tutted to himself as he looked at the wound; I was not relieved by the sound. He then leaned down to take a deep sniff. *Is he checking me for gangrene or something?* He stood up and reapplied that bandage as well.

"You're pretty lucky, Mr. Smith," he said around the cigarette. *Smith? Who's Mr. Smith?* He took the cigarette out of his mouth and pointed at my shoulder with it. "That dog bite doesn't look so bad." *Dog bite?* I gave Agent Wright a quizzical look and he merely shrugged his shoulders.

"But that stomach wound looks worse," the doctor continued. "How long have you had it?"

I shrugged, looking at Agent Wright for guidance. Receiving none, I said, "A couple of days, I guess?"

"How'd you get it?"

"Umm...a neighbor's dog bit me," I lied. It was interesting how easily the lies were coming to me now. *I must be hanging out with the wrong sort of people.*

"You may want to check to make sure it's not rabid or something." The doctor pointed again with his cigarette, but to my stomach wound this time. "That wound's not healing like it should. It's not septic yet, but we need to keep an eye on it to make sure that it doesn't get any worse." He picked up my chart and made some notations on it.

"We're going to keep you here overnight," said the doctor, looking up from the chart. "Just to keep an eye on you. I want to make sure that there's no infection in your shoulder and to see if your stomach wound looks any better in the morning." He hung the chart on a peg at the foot of my bed. "Have a good night," he nodded to Agent Wright as he left the room.

The nurse followed him out of the room and I was left alone with Agent Wright. "So what now?" I asked him.

"I don't know." He shrugged and rubbed his hand across a day's growth of stubble. He looked as tired as I felt. "We had hoped that your girlfriend would have been able to help us, maybe even give us a lead on Capone that we might be able to use. Now, I don't know. Without her we don't have anything."

"Do you think Capone's a...you know." I couldn't

bring myself to say the word right now.

"I'm not sure. Until now I would have said no, even though his ruthlessness and ability to charm pretty much anybody seems to fit with what we do know about vampires." He shrugged again. "But no mention of it has shown up in any of our files and we've never heard even a whisper from any of our informants. Maybe it's all just a coincidence."

"I don't believe in coincidence," Agent Truesdale said walking into the room. "He's one of them. I can feel it in my gut."

He turned and looked at me. "So, you gonna live or what?"

I guess that was Truesdale's way of caring. I nodded. My body ached all over, and the bandages were starting to itch, so I figured that meant that I was going to live.

"Good. Stay that way." Agent Truesdale turned to leave.

"Wait. I need some answers," I demanded.

Agent Truesdale stopped in the doorway. "No, you don't," he said in his gruff voice.

"The hell I don't!" I shot back. "The reason I'm here is because Moira attacked me. She was going to kill me!"

Agent Truesdale looked up at the ceiling for a moment, then turned around and crossed his arms as if to say, "So what?"

"Moira accused me of talking to the Feds and told me that the Feds had arrested Ralph Capone. So, that means that somebody knew that I met with the two of you. She told me that she was sent by her 'master' to kill me because of Ralph's arrest! So since I assume that you two went and arrested Ralph, then it's your fuckin' fault that I'm in here! I think I deserve to know what the fuck is going on!" I ended my tirade practically yelling, causing a passing nurse to stick her head into the room.

"What's going on here?" she asked. "The doctor has given strict orders for this patient to not be disturbed."

Agent Wright pulled out his wallet and showed her his badge. With a smile he said, "We're almost done here ma'am," before politely pushing her out of the room and closing the door. He then turned around and asked, "Did she tell you who her master was?"

"No! And I was too busy getting my ass kicked to ask!"

"That's too bad. That could have been useful information." Wright sounded disappointed that I'd not thought to ask Moira who her master was during our fight. *It's not like we had been on a date and making small talk.* I hadn't had time to think about anything while I was trying to keep her from killing me. I gave him a look that said "go shove it up your ass". I was getting tired of being everybody's pawn.

"Look, Saul," Agent Wright said. "It's better that you don't know what is going on. You'll be in less danger that way."

I gave him an incredulous look. "I was almost killed by my girlfriend tonight because of what you two are doing. How can I be in less danger?"

Truesdale chimed in. "All you need to do is what we tell you to do, got it?" He jabbed a meaty finger toward me. "Agent Wright and I have everything under control."

"Okay, so I guess I'll just lay here while you two *hit-sigers* go and arrest Al Capone's brother and piss off the biggest gangster in all of Chicago." They were acting like hotheads, flying by the seat of their pants and with no care for the consequences.

Truesdale actually smiled and nodded. "All part of the plan, kid." He turned, opened the door, and they left the room.

Chapter 27

I had a hard time falling asleep. To begin with, my body was now so used to my work schedule that it was rebelling at the fact that I was trying to sleep when it knew that I should be awake and sorting mail. More importantly though, my arm, back, and chest all hurt like hell. Since the doctor thought I had only been attacked by a 'dog', all they had given me for the pain was some aspirin. It had worked for about an hour, but then the pain had come roaring back.

I lay on the bed in my dark room, staring up at the ceiling. There was a single window that looked out on one of the streets and the city light leaked in around the closed curtains. Some light from the hallway seeped in under the door and from the open window above it.

Since I couldn't sleep, I kept replaying the events of the past few days over and over in my mind. I kept trying to remember if there had been any clues that Moira was a vampire, and I kept striking out. When I thought about Moira, I only remembered everything good about her; how we met, our first date at the Green Mill, the events on St. Valentine's Day and all the wild events since that fateful day. I relived our lovemaking—there was a nagging feeling in the back of my mind that I should have known something was different with Moira that day—the way that she had acted by biting me and playing with the blood. But I challenge any guy to think straight or clear-headed when in the middle of having sex, even kinky sex. It can't be done.

What bothered me the most was what she had said during our fight. *"You had such promise, Saul."* I could hear her voice in my head. During the fight she had sounded full of anger and rage, but now, in my mind, she sounded disappointed. *"You were going to be my ace in the hole, my ticket to freedom, but now I'm forced to destroy my own creation or be killed myself. Such a fucking waste."*

Destroy my own creation. Ice began to form in my stomach as I let those words sink in. Unconsciously, my right hand drifted down to the first bite wound Moira had given me. I racked my brain trying to remember everything that Agent Wright had said about vampires. He said that they had to feed on their victim at the neck. But what if he was wrong? What if they just needed to feed, period? Then I heard Mr. Brown's voice in my head, *"And the Gusenbergs were completing their 'rights' to become brothers as well. Had they completed the process then Frank might have survived."*

Did that mean they had to feed multiple times to make a new vampire? Maybe. I was just making a guess since Mr. Brown never really said that they would have become vampires, but the pieces were starting to fit together. I sighed with relief. Moira had only bitten me that one time—not counting tonight—and I didn't think that this shoulder wound counted.

I started to relax. Then I heard Mrs. Rabinowitz's voice in my head. *"But why did she come back later?"* I recalled the conversation we had on the second floor landing by her door on the morning after Agent Truesdale had given me my black eye. She said that she'd seen Moira come to my apartment while I'd been asleep. *"... she didn't stay long as she left a few minutes after arriving. Did the two of you get into a scuffle? It looked like her lips were bleeding."*

Dread flowed through my veins, chilling me to my core. "Shit, shit, shit." I muttered to myself. *What the hell is going on? Am I going to become a raving monster– a creature of the night? Or is the process not finished? How many times does a vampire need to feed to make a new vampire? Two? Three? More? What happens if the process isn't completed?*

My only knowledge of vampires came from reading *Dracula* and what Agent Wright had told me. I didn't consider either source to be very reliable on the subject.

I continued to fret and worry about this problem until my eyes finally grew heavy. I must have eventually dozed off since I dreamed, reliving Moira's attack and our fight. I kept trying to tell Moira that I hadn't done anything wrong, but she sneered and stuck a straw in me, which she used to drink my blood. As she drank, I could feel my body pulsing and changing, until I had transformed into a hideous, hunched beast with long claws and fangs. Moira laughed and called me to heel like a dog, her faithful pet, and I dutifully moved to her side, panting and nuzzling her thigh. She reached down and grabbed the back of my neck and I felt pain shoot through my body. I was paralyzed as she leaned down and bit into my neck. The feeling of her biting me was simultaneously excruciatingly painful and blissfully orgasmic. My body shook, and I woke up with a start.

Cold, damp sweat soaked my clothes and sheets. I looked around and saw nothing in the dim light, but somehow I could sense that I was not alone in the room. "Who's there?" I called out.

"My my, Mr. Imbierowicz, that must have been quite the dream."

I recognized Bugs Moran's voice and, as I turned toward the sound, there was the click of a lamp. Moran was sitting in a chair next to the window. The lights from the lamp and the city cast an eerie glow on his face. At first I was embarrassed that he had seen me dreaming, then my embarrassment was replaced with confusion and anger. "How did you know I was here?"

"Now, now," he chuckled. "The Beast isn't the only one with connections in this town. When I heard that you had been so viciously attacked I knew that I had to come down here to show my concern." He leaned down and there was the flare of a lighter as he lit a cigar.

"I'm glad I mean so much to you," I replied. I didn't try to hide the sarcasm.

" I thought we had a deal, Saul." Moran paused to blow out a plume of smoke. "You made a deal with me to get me those books. But today, I hear that the Feds went and arrested Ralph Capone." His voice was quiet, but held more menace because of it.

"What do you mean?" I asked. "Isn't that what you wanted? Ralph got arrested, so that must be good for you and your operation."

Moran laughed a harsh, dry laugh. "Saul, you *schmuck*. I don't care whether Ralphie was arrested or not. That's not the point. You went and involved the wrong people." He jabbed his cigar toward me. *Great*, I thought. *First Moira and now Moran.* "You went and got the Feds involved and they fucked everything up. They don't know shit, and they certainly don't know how we do things here in Chicago."

I shook my head. I really didn't understand, and getting blamed a second time for going to see Agents Truesdale and Wright was starting to irritate me. "I don't understand. Isn't it *good* that Ralph Capone was arrested? Isn't that just as good as having the books?"

"You're a fuckin' idiot, Saul. Putting Ralph in the hands of the Feds doesn't give me the leverage that I need to twist Big Al's tail in order to get him to do what I want him to do. The books are the only thing that will give me that leverage, and will allow me to tell Capone where he can shove that small dick of his. But that chance is blown, now, because you had to run and cry to the fuckin' Feds."

I sat there in my bed trying to understand what Moran was telling me. None of this was making any sense. "I didn't know what they were going to do. It's not like they told me their plans."

"Well, the cops who were holding onto Ralph let him out earlier today due to a lack of evidence." Moran seemed reflective. He turned, pulled open the curtain, and looked out across Chicago. His thinking had me worried.

"This was a deal between you and me, Saul. We had a simple understanding and now you've broken my trust. And if you can't trust your friends," Moran turned and looked at me, "who can you trust?"

Wait, friends? When had we ever been friends? "Look," I said, my voice cracking a bit. "I can still get the books for you."

"No, Saul," Moran moved toward the door. "It's too late for that. Now I have to take care of it myself."

Chapter 28

The stink of Moran's cigar lingered in the room, along with his parting words, which rang and bounced around in my head. My biggest fear was that he was going to take out his anger with me on my family. I felt so helpless. If he was going after my parents and sister, what could I do about it? I leaned my head back against the pillow and sighed. I was powerless to do anything; even if I hadn't been hurt, what could I do to stop Moran if he decided to take out my family?

As I lay there in the dark, I recalled Moran's last words. *"Now I have to take care of it myself."* I wondered if he might have meant something other than hurting my family, but I couldn't think of anything else. Images of Moran's goons—Cup and Glass—bursting into my parent's house with Tommy Guns blazing away kept filling my mind.

After a few minutes of this torture, I had had enough. I sat up, wincing at the pain in my chest and shoulder. I flung off my covers and started to get out of bed. My body ached all over and, as I stood up, new pain rippled up my back from all of my wounds. I looked around for some clothes—nothing. I seemed to recall that they had cut off my bloody clothes and thrown them away when I had been brought in for treatment. I cursed my luck and headed toward the door.

Just then, the door opened and a nurse walked in. "What in God's name do you think you are doing?" Her voice might have sounded nice, except for the fact that she sounded just like my mother when she caught me stealing cookies before dinner.

"I need to go home," I said.

"Not a chance, young man." I blushed a bit at being called 'young man'. She couldn't have been more than a couple of years older than me, and wasn't half bad to gaze at. She hurried across the room and guided me back into bed. I wanted to resist, but my mom taught me better than to be mean to a lady (vampires notwithstanding). "You can't leave until the doctor has had a chance to look at you in the morning."

"When will that be?"

"Oh, he usually gets in around 9 o'clock." She finished tucking me back into the bed, making sure that the covers bound me tightly to the mattress. "Now you stay in bed, dear."

She gave my bandages a once-over, and stuck a thermometer in my mouth for good measure while she took my pulse. She pulled the thermometer out and read it carefully. Satisfied, she wrote some stuff on my chart and left the room.

I lay there, staring up at the ceiling, feeling even worse than I had before.

It felt like an eternity had passed before I saw the first rays of sunlight creep around the window shade. What little sleep I got was consistently shattered by dreams of Moran taking his revenge on my family. I anxiously waited while another eternity passed before the doctor finally came in. He poked at my wounds, pulling off the bandages and feeling around. I winced at the pain but managed to swallow the yelps and cries as he poked and prodded. He pried open my mouth with a tongue depressor, then squeezed my neck and shone a penlight into my eyes. He grunted a few times, and scribbled a few things on my chart. Apparently finished, he left without ever saying a word.

I was about to get up again when the door opened and a new nurse walked in. She was older, and less appealing to look at, but she was carrying some clothes with her, which made her the loveliest person in the whole world.

"Here you go, honey. Your friend left these here for you last night. The doctor says you can be released." She laid the clothes on the bed and I immediately grabbed them to start getting dressed. The nurse quickly averted her eyes and left the room.

It took me five times longer than normal to get dressed, and it hurt like hell, but I finally got all my clothes on. I headed out the door, finding my way to the elevator and then out of the hospital. I was initially a bit pissed that Truesdale and Wright weren't there to meet me, but on second thought, they probably would have insisted on babysitting me.

It took me a minute to get my bearings, then I headed for the nearest L station. Truesdale or Wright—probably Wright as he was certainly the nicer of the two Agents—had left me some money in my pocket. I took the train back to my old neighborhood, and walked (I was in too much pain to run) as fast as I could to my parent's apartment building.

I saw a strange car in front of their building, and I immediately thought the worst. Moran's thugs had gotten here before I could do anything. A rock-hard lump of bile formed in my stomach as I continued to approach the apartment. As I got closer, I saw that the car had a name stenciled on the side: Schofield's Flower Shop. This made me even more worried—Schofield's was known to have been owned by Dean O'Banion, who was the leader of the North Side Gang until his death five years ago. Some people said that Moran still used the flower shop as a front.

As I neared the steps to the apartment, a young delivery man came out of the building, tipping his hat to me as he walked down the steps. I was torn between racing upstairs to my parent's place and decking this hired killer right here and now. My left hand flexed and tightened into a fist, but some doubt in my mind stayed my hand. Instead, I just glared at the delivery man as he got into the car and drove off.

I headed inside and went up the stairs. As soon as I limped onto my parent's floor, my worries and fears all melted away as I could hear Mom yelling at Sarah. I couldn't make out the words, but I didn't need to. Just hearing the raised voices, arguing over something mundane, told me that they were safe—at least from Moran. I knew Dad would be at the packing plant, and there was no way any of Moran's goons would be able to get in there.

I was about to open the door, when a shooting pain in my shoulder reminded me that I was not exactly in the best state to be seen by my mother. There was no lie I could tell Mom that could explain away my bruises, cuts, and other wounds. She would be merciless in her questions and I would eventually have to explain everything to her. I would rather have faced Moira again than face my Mom right now.

With a twinge of reluctance, I turned and headed back down the stairs.

I got back to my apartment around noon. I climbed the stairs to my floor slowly, the sounds of my fight with Moira yesterday echoing in my head. I was not looking forward to being back at my place and seeing the aftermath of what had happened. I know that she had turned into some kind of monster and had tried to kill me, but a small part of me still loved Moira. To come back and see all the blood and everything might be more than I could bear right now.

I shook my head to clear it as I reached the third floor landing. My door was there, shut, and as I tried the handle, I found that it was also locked. Part of me marvelled at that little fact as I patted my pockets and found a single key in one of them. I put the key in the lock and opened the door.

I was shocked by what I saw or, more appropriately, what I didn't see. My kitchen was so clean that it practically glowed. There was no sign of the bloody fight. Had I not known differently, I would have sworn that Mom had been over here and had cleaned the place up.

The floor was freshly scrubbed and smelled of bleach. All of the walls had been scrubbed as well. There was not a trace of blood anywhere. The table had been cleaned and set upright, and a new chair sat at the table to replace the one that had ended Moira's life.

I looked into my room and saw that the blood had been cleaned from the floor and wall in there as well, and that the bed had been made. I went back into the kitchen and found a note sitting under my coffee cup on the counter.

"I hope that everything looks like it did before the accident. Call us. ~ Wright"

I looked around again and shook my head in disbelief. I idly wondered if I could somehow get them to come back to clean my bathroom, too?

I was pondering this when there was a knock on my door. I jumped at the sound. I couldn't remember the last time somebody had actually knocked in order to gain entry to my apartment. I walked over and opened the door.

Al Capone stood on the landing, looking immaculate in a dark blue suit and white silk shirt and wearing a black fur coat that made his slightly large body seem even bigger. He had on a dark blue and gold-striped tie and was wearing a pearl-grey, snap-brimmed fedora with a blue silk band. He looked at me expectantly. "May I come in, Mr. Imbierowicz?"

Chapter 29

I hesitated slightly looking at the man standing in my doorway. His face was puffy and slightly red-faced and I could just make out his namesake scar. My first instinct was to slam the door in his face. Luckily, I thought better of it before I acted. "Uh...please come in, Mr. Capone." I swung my arm to usher him into my kitchen.

Capone took a confident step and walked into my apartment, taking off his hat and holding it in his gloved hands. He looked around with a flat expression. I felt a bit self-conscious as he looked over my simple apartment with the shabby and sparse furnishings.

"This reminds me of the small place my wife and I had when we first moved to Chicago," Capone said, with nostalgia. "It was above the Four Deuces, where I worked as a bouncer. I would come home after a long day, to an apartment almost like this, and kiss my wife and bounce my son on my knee."

I wasn't sure what to say to that; I was shocked that Al Capone was revealing such private information to me. I decided it was better to keep my mouth shut.

Capone walked around the kitchen, first looking into the living room and then my bedroom. It was a bit unnerving, like he was putting me under a microscope. I hadn't had this feeling since my Mom had come over to see my apartment right after I had moved in. At least

Capone didn't pull out a handkerchief like Mom did to run along the baseboards.

"What can I do for you, Mr. Capone?" I finally asked.

Capone stopped in the entryway into my bedroom and turned, his steel-grey eyes boring into me. "Did you know that Moira was one of the first people I met when I came to Chicago? Hmmm?"

I shook my head dumbly.

"I was most upset at learning about her passing. She was special to me. She'd worked in one of the brothels before I saved her." He looked almost wistfully toward the ceiling, as if recalling a favorite memory.

"Did she ever mention that? Her past? She worked in one of the sleaziest whorehouses in all of Chicago. I bet she must have spread her legs for half the men in the city." He looked at me as if expecting an answer, but my mouth had gone dry. I could feel my hands clenching into fists. I wanted to remember Moira as I knew her, not as the whore that Capone was making her out to be. Capone must have seen me clenching my fists since he gave me a sneering grin.

"No? She learned much during her time there, and with my gift she was able to use that experience to her full advantage. She always had an independent streak, and she could be a wild one in bed, as I'm sure you know." He gave me a knowing smile, and I felt bile rise in my throat as I realized that Moira and Capone had been lovers. "And she never failed me at anything, ever. That is, before she met you. Why is that, do you suppose?" His voice almost purred and he raised a questioning eyebrow, but he didn't give me time to respond. I was starting to wonder what the hell Capone wanted. *Why had he come to my place?*

"Moira may have been a bit too independent. Sure, I could control her, but she was always fighting, straining at the bit to get free. In a way, I guess I should thank you for killing her. I would have had to have done it eventually, and it would have hurt me here," he patted his chest, "to do it, but I would have done it. Do you know why?" Capone gave me a piercing look.

"I would have killed Moira myself because she wasn't family. Family is important. Wouldn't you agree, Mr. Imbierowicz, that family is important?"

I nodded, not liking where this conversation was going. *Oh shit.*

Capone walked back to the center of the kitchen, resting a gloved hand on the back of my new chair. "My family is very important to me. My wife and son, my mother. My brothers, too. All of them are important to me." He gave me another piercing look. I couldn't have spoken, even though I had nothing to say.

"Yesterday, the Feds arrested my brother Ralph. They pulled him from his home before dawn, in front of his wife and kids, like a common criminal." Capone made a dismissive gesture with his hat. "That didn't worry me too much. The cops have done that sort of thing in the past and the Feds didn't have anything they could make stick. In fact, Ralph was out of jail and back home by lunch."

Capone paused, looking down at his shoes. "Then, this morning, when Ralph was heading to work, somebody had the gall to drive by his house, shooting up the peaceful morning and filling the air with lead."

"Thats-" The word escaped from my mouth without thought. I now knew what Moran had meant by his parting words in my hospital room early this morning.

"Tragic, yes," said Capone, thankfully misinterpreting my statement. "Luckily for Ralph—and his family—the shooter didn't know what the hell he was doing. Every shot missed. Nobody got hurt."

"Oh, thank God." Again, the words came without my thinking about them. I instantly regretted it since it sounded like I was more relieved for myself than I was for Ralph. Capone seemed to sense my relief.

"You'll be thanking Him in person tomorrow if you don't get me those fuckin' books!" Capone's voice suddenly boomed and echoed around my kitchen, his face coloring as he jabbed a finger at me. "I want those books, and I fuckin' want them tonight!" He paused and straightened his suit and tie and put the fedora back on. His face relaxed a bit and I swear that I saw fangs receding back into his mouth.

"You will get the books and deliver them to me tonight," Capone's voice was softer now, more under control. "Or tomorrow morning a similar shooter will come by as your pop is walking to the meat packing plant, and another will visit your mom and sister at their apartment. I can assure you that my gunmen know exactly what they are doing, and by this time tomorrow you will be looking for a good undertaker for your whole family."

"S-s-sure thing," I said. My heart was racing and my stomach felt like it was in my throat. "I will get the books for you tonight. How do I contact you?"

Capone turned and opened the door. "Call on me at the Lexington." He headed out the door, closing it softly behind him.

Chapter 30

I stared at the door for a couple of minutes after Capone had left, unsure as to what to do next. My situation really hadn't changed since Capone still expected me to get the books. I wasn't sure anymore if Moran still expected me to get them for him as well, or if he'd satisfied his anger by taking a shot at Ralph. Whether he did or not, I only had one real course of action available to me if I wanted to try and keep my parents and sister alive. I went downstairs to the phone and called the Feds.

"Bureau of Investigations," said the familiar voice on the other end of the phone.

"Wright," I said. "It's Saul."

"Hey, Saul. You make it home from the hospital alright?"

"Yeah, but I've had a couple of visitors since we last talked." I explained for a couple of minutes about the visit that I'd received from Moran last night, and then my encounter with Capone just now. Wright was silent while I talked.

"I need to get the books for Capone," I said, once I'd finished. "It's the only thing that will make Capone happy and make it so that my parents and sister don't end up dead."

There was silence on the other end. After a minute I couldn't stand the lack of noise. "Wright, are you still there?"

"I'm here," came a gruff reply. Wright must have handed the phone to Truesdale. "Listen, kid. Get your ass to work tonight like normal. We've got everything sorted out. Whenever we contact you, you need to be ready to do whatever the fuck we tell you to do."

"What about the books? I don't care about anything else, I just want to make sure that my family is safe."

"Again with the family," Truesdale said in a commanding voice. "I told you, we've got it sorted out." He slammed the receiver down.

I stared at the phone for a moment, worried that my family's lives were now in the hands of Agents Truesdale and Wright. I shuddered. I hung up the phone and went back upstairs. Unfortunately, I ran into Mrs. Rabinowitz as she came out of her apartment. "My goodness, Saul! Look at all those bandages. Are you sure you're alright after that burglar broke in yesterday?" She stared at me and I realized that I must have looked horrible just with the bruises and bandages that were showing.

"Yes, Mrs. R," I said. "It's really just a few scratches and bumps. The doctors were just being overly protective."

Mrs. R. gave me the same look that Mom had given me as a kid whenever I told her one of my lies. She pursed her lips and narrowed her eyes, but then nodded slightly. "Well, I hope you have gotten a second lock put on your door now, Saul."

"Yes ma'am." I wasn't in the mood to have this conversation again. I tried to move past her and up the stairs.

"Oh, Saul."

"Yes, Mrs. Rabinowitz," I sighed.

"That nice young girl you've been seeing," Mrs. R. reached out and patted my arm and smiled. "When are you going to take her home to meet your mother?"

Yeah, that's not going to happen. Even if Moira had still been alive, how would I have introduced a vampire to my mother? "Soon," I lied again.

"That's good," Mrs. R. said. "I'm sure that your mother would really like her." She headed down the stairs.

I continued upstairs to my apartment. I shut and locked my door, double checking the lock for some reason. I went to the bedroom and looked at the clock. It was just after 2 p.m. I laid down on the bed and set the alarm but, even as exhausted as I was, I was too wound up to sleep. I didn't know what was going to happen in the next few hours, and thoughts that my family's lives were now in the Feds hands kept me wide awake. I really didn't know if Truesdale and Wright were in this to help me and save my family, or were just trying to find out if Capone was some vampire gang leader.

I finally gave up on trying to go to sleep. I got out of bed and drew a bath. I managed to get plenty of hot water and gave myself a nice bath. My wounds stung in the hot water, and the bruises that I could see on my legs and stomach were turning an ugly yellow-green color. My 'love bite' from Moira was still raw. It looked like the doctor and nurse had managed to clean it up some but, as I touched it, fresh blood still oozed from the wound. It had an ugly look to it; the skin around the wound was turning a green-black color, like the skin was dying.

I realized that there wasn't a damn thing I could do about it. I couldn't worry about myself right now. I finished cleaning up, got out of the bath, shaved, and dressed for work. The sun was just setting as I left the apartment. I walked downstairs and headed up the street to the L. The air was very cold; I could see small crystals forming around me as I walked and there was a smell of snow in the air.

I got off the L and walked down to the Post Office. I was several hours early for my shift so I walked into the diner to have dinner. I didn't recognize either the waitress or cook who worked the evening shift, which was fine with me. I didn't want to have to talk to anybody right now. I ordered dinner—meatloaf, mashed potatoes, and carrots—and coffee. When my meal arrived, I picked at the food but didn't feel like eating. I couldn't remember the last meal that I'd eaten but I wasn't really hungry. I guess that I had too many butterflies flittering around in my stomach. I ended up just pushing the food around on my plate, eating an occasional bite. Eventually, the food got cold and I gave up on the thought of eating.

I did drink a lot of coffee, and I got a nasty look from the waitress when she gave me my fourth coffee refill, but I didn't care. There were too many thoughts running around in my head. Would the Feds be able to save my family? Was I becoming a vampire?

Mostly, I just thought about getting my hands on those damn books and if, once I had them, they would be enough to satisfy Capone and keep him from going after my family.

Chapter 31

At around 9:45 I finally got up from the booth and paid for my food. I even gave the waitress a dime tip, but I don't think that she was very happy that I'd taken up space in her booth all night. I walked out through the lobby, past the information booth, and took the elevators up to the third floor. I clocked in and was busy at my station sorting mail when Joe arrived. He gave me a look of surprise. "Hey Saul, I'm surprised to see you here. When you missed work yesterday I figured you'd either gotten run over or fired."

"The former," I said.

Joe turned and gave me a look like I was pulling his leg, then paused as he took in my various bruises and cuts. "Shit, Saul. What the hell happened to you?"

I was just about to tell him when I saw Mr. Dickenson, the shift supervisor, walking over. "Mr. Imbierowicz," he said. "I hope that you have sufficiently recovered from your accident and that you are able to work. The detectives explained everything, so I will forgive your absence yesterday, but I can't have you shirking your duties. If you miss any more work I will have to terminate you."

"Yes, sir," I said. "I'm fine. There won't be any problems."

Mr. Dickenson gave me a look; I'm sure he was looking at my black eye and the bandage that poked out from under the collar of my shirt. He seemed to be satisfied with my answer and walked back to his office. I looked over at Joe, who said, "So, spill the beans. What the hell happened to you?"

I grabbed a stack of envelopes and winced a bit from the pain in my shoulder as I started to sort the mail. "It was dumb, man. I was walking home from work the other morning when this big dog just started chasing me for no reason. I would have outrun it, but I slipped on some ice and the damn thing bit me on the shoulder." I pointed to my right shoulder with a stack of envelopes.

"Man, that must have hurt."

"No shit!" That was certainly not a lie. It had hurt like hell when Moira had bitten me.

"Seems sorta odd that it would bite you on the shoulder."

"Huh?"

"Well, you'd think that a dog would bite you on the leg, or the arm, or something. If you were trying to fend it off."

"Well, you try fending off a ferocious beast when you've fallen on your ass. It's harder than you'd think."

Joe shrugged, but seemed to be satisfied by my answer and we went back to sorting the mail. The job was mind-numbingly boring, but Joe and I kept up enough chatter about nothing in particular that the time seemed to go by pretty quickly. At around midnight, Mr. Dickenson let everyone take a ten minute smoke break. We weren't allowed to smoke in the sorting room as there was too much risk that a burning cigarette might start a fire. Joe and I headed out into the hallway, along with about three-quarters of the rest of the staff. Everybody broke into little groups of friends as they lit up their Luckies, Chesterfields, and Morleys. Joe and I headed down the hall to a spot we used, generally away from the others. It was by one of the large windows and looked out toward the city and the lake beyond.

I pulled out my pack of Chesterfields and my Ronson, lighting up a cigarette as we leaned against the window ledge. There was a flare of a match from Joe as he lit up his own Morley. I looked out the window and wondered what was taking Truesdale so long. It was after midnight and I'd not heard a peep from him. *I knew I shouldn't have listened to him.*

"So, why did the cops get involved?" Joe asked as he blew out a puff of smoke.

"Huh?" I was so wrapped up in my own thoughts that I was caught off guard by the question and, at first, I didn't know exactly what he was talking about.

"Your dog bite," he pointed at my shoulder with his hand, cigarette lightly held between two fingers. "Why'd the cops get involved?"

I took a pull on my own cigarette to stall. *Why did Joe have to be so nosy?* I thought maybe I could lie and avoid the question.

"What cops?" I asked innocently. "I didn't need any cops for a dog bite."

"Mr. Dickenson said earlier that some detectives came by to tell him why you weren't at work last night. Why would the cops be needed for a stupid dog bite?"

Joe took another drag on his cigarette, the flare of the tip casting a red glow to his face. I was immediately on edge by his question. Joe had always been a nosy SOB, but he was never this pointed, or this observant, in his questions.

"I'm just glad they helped out otherwise I wouldn't be here to have this dumb conversation with you." I tried to make it sound like I was joking with Joe, hoping that he'd drop the subject. "Does it matter?" I asked, not trying to hide the exasperation from my voice.

Joe shrugged and took another pull on his cigarette. "I guess not," he admitted. He looked out the window, the lights of the city giving him a pale, washed out look. I turned to look at the clock in the hallway. *Come on, Truesdale. What's taking you so long?* I could feel my stomach churning as I watched the second hand sweep by on the clock. *Truesdale is going to leave me hanging here, and I'm going to find my family's corpses when I get off work. He never cared about me or my family. Why did I ever trust him?*

"How's Moira?" Joe asked.

"What?" The question shocked me out of my reverie and I dropped my cigarette onto my pants. "Oh, crap." I batted at the spot to wipe away the ash and bent to pick up the cigarette.

Joe laughed at my clumsiness, "Man, are you some kind of *klutz*. How's your girlfriend doing?"

"Fine, fine," I said. I wasn't about to tell Joe that I had shoved a chair leg through her chest.

"You know, you really ought to be careful around her."

I froze and looked at Joe. What the hell was he talking about?

"I don't think you know what you are getting yourself into with her." He looked at me with an expression that was a mix of stern parent and concerned friend.

I was about to ask him what he meant when Mr. Dickenson walked up and cleared his throat, catching us both by surprise. "Final warning, gentlemen," he said. "Next time I will dock your pay."

Joe and I stubbed our cigarettes out in the ashtray and hurried back into the sorting room. There was a fresh box of letters for each of us, and Mr. Dickenson felt that he had to stand around watching us to make sure that we didn't slack off any more. With him around, I couldn't ask Joe anything about what he had meant by his comment about Moira. Every time I looked over at Joe he just ignored me.

After about 30 minutes Mr. Dickenson finally left, but by this time I had gotten so busy with the sorting that I forgot about Joe. My thoughts kept coming back to Capone and my family. Horrible images of Capone laughing maniacally while shooting my mom and sister with a Tommy Gun kept flashing through my mind. I looked up at the clock every chance I got and it seemed like it was barely moving. At one point I swore that I even saw the second hand tick backwards. "What's taking so long?" I mumbled.

Joe must have heard me, "Relax, man." He was leaning against the sorting table. "They'll have our next baskets of mail soon enough. Why the rush?"

I looked down and realized that Joe was right. Somehow I had managed to get through the basket of mail without realizing it. I tried to laugh it off. "No reason," I said. "I just feel like time goes faster when we're working, ya know."

"Don't I know it." As was usually the case, this got Joe started in on how he'd worked a job as a kid waiting to run messages for somebody and how the hours would drag by when there weren't any messages to deliver.

I was absently listening as two more baskets of mail

were rolled up, one for each of us. I reached in and grabbed the first thing on top: a large, thick package wrapped in brown paper and tied with a string. I took a look for the address but didn't see anything. I flipped it over and saw that a piece of paper had been pinned to the package.

S—Here they are. Call C and tell him to meet you at the Michigan Ave. bridge at 2 a.m. We'll take care of the rest. T

My heart was racing. I had the books right here. I was holding them in my hands, and that meant that my parents would be safe. I glanced up at the clock. 1:15. *Shit*, I thought. *Not much time.*

Without saying anything, I turned and walked away from the sorting table. "Saul?" Joe's voice called from behind me. "Saul, what are you doin'? Dickenson will fire you."

I ignored him and walked out of the sorting room. I hurried and ran down the stairs, taking them two at a time. I reached the main floor and ran into the diner, where I knew there was a phone. I raced in past Francine without acknowledging her surprise at seeing me and grabbed the phone. The operator asked me for the number.

"Lexington Hotel," I said.

There was a pause and I heard several clicks as the call was connected. Out of the corner of my eye I could see Francine looking at me curiously, but I ignored her. I heard the phone ring three times before it was answered. "Lexington Hotel, front desk," said a voice that was way too polite for this time of the night.

"Please connect me with Al Capone."

"One moment." There was no back talk or questions, like Al Capone always got phone calls at one-thirty in the morning.

I waited for only a few seconds before I heard Capone's distinct voice. "Mr. Imbierowicz," his voice was silky smooth. "So good of you to call. I hope you have something for me?"

"Yes," I said, hefting the package in my hand. "I have them. I will meet you at the Michigan Avenue Bridge in half an hour to deliver them to you."

"That seems a bit presumptuous of you." Capone's voice was steely and threatening. "Why not bring them to me here?"

Shit. Capone will insist on me coming to the hotel. But maybe that works for me? I can give him the books and my family will be safe from him. But what about Moran, damnit? If I give Capone the books, Moran may still be pissed at me and take out my family. Shit. I still needed Truesdale and whatever his damn plan is to get through this. *Ok, how do I get Capone to meet me at the bridge?*

"Look," I said, "I can't get away long enough to get them up to the hotel. The bridge is closer, and that way nobody will see what we are doing." I was thinking on my feet here, but I thought that sounded pretty good.

Capone must have felt that way too. "I suppose that does make sense. Fine, I will meet you at the bridge in thirty minutes." The line clicked off.

Chapter 32

Twenty-five minutes later I was standing in the middle of Wacker Drive, my hands clutching the package as I stared at the bridge on Michigan Avenue. The city was quiet at this time of the morning and a light snow was falling, with the flakes glittering in the lights around the bridge. The temperature was very cold and a light wind was blowing up the river from Lake Michigan. My breath wreathed my head in a cloud of fog. I glanced around to see if I could spot Truesdale or Wright, wondering if they were even going to show up. *Are they going to leave me hanging here to face Capone by myself?* No, this was where Truesdale wanted Capone and me, so I knew that they had to be nearby, even if I couldn't see them.

I walked over to the bridge, the snowflakes tickling my cheeks. I glanced at the carving on the bridge house depicting a man, sword drawn, his left arm grabbing at an Indian. The sculpture was titled Defense and represented the Battle of Fort Dearborn. I shrugged my shoulders, hoping that it was an auspicious sign as I was doing my best to defend my family.

Sounds of a car pulling up behind me caused me to turn around. I watched as a dark green Cadillac pulled up and parked on Wacker. The car sat there idling for a few seconds, then the engine turned off. Al Capone stepped out from the driver's seat and closed the door.

Capone was wearing a black suit with a white shirt and black bow tie. He was wearing diamond cufflinks that glittered like fire in the street lights. Draped across his shoulders was a black cape with a red silk lining and a fur-trimmed collar. It looked like he was dressed for the opera.

I moved out to the center of Michigan Avenue, taking a few involuntary steps backward onto the bridge. My footsteps rang loudly on the metal plating. I shivered, and it wasn't because of the cold.

Capone took a moment to put on some white gloves, looked left and right, then looked up the street and across the bridge. Satisfied, he stepped away from the car toward the bridge.

"Good evening, Mr. Imbierowicz." He smiled politely, but I could tell that it wasn't genuine. His eyes never left mine and they held a predatory glint. "Did you bring my package?"

Numbly, I held out the bundle. "Here it is," I said. "It's yours. Now please tell me that you'll leave my family alone."

Capone held up a hand. "Not until I have made sure that this is the genuine article." He took a step forward and I handed the package to him. "You know, Mr. Imbierowicz, I have been most unhappy with how difficult it has been for me to get these back. It should have been a simple thing for Moira to play her charms on you and for you to get the books and give them to her. I still don't know exactly what happened there, but I have a theory. Would you like to hear it?" Capone held the package but didn't move to open it. I wanted to tell him to get on with it, but I was a bit curious myself ever since he'd come to my apartment.

"I told you before that Moira worked for me, and that I made her. I made her in the same sense that Johnny Torrio made me. Johnny warned me not to, you know. He felt that she was too independent, but I was new to my 'profession' and I didn't listen to his counsel. She died in my arms, willingly, and was reborn as one of us, one of the undead." He gave me a look and I saw his eyes glow with a reddish light, as if stoked by an inner fire.

A frozen lump formed in the pit of my stomach. *Shit.* Al Capone just told me that he's a vampire. He'd made Moira into a vampire as well. I know that in the back of my mind that I had suspected this, but now it was confirmed. I took a hesitant step back and started to sweat despite the freezing temperatures.

"Moira should have done my bidding without hesitation, but I think she wanted out. I could feel her struggling against me, fighting my control. You see, I knew she had met with Moran. I think she was trying to use him to get to me. I don't know what she told him, but Moran was trying to get some of his own men." Capone gave me a hard look. "Men like me. I think he was doing it with Moira's help. That's why I ordered the attack at the garage last week. I couldn't have Moran getting his hands on vampire goons," Capone chuckled. "It would have upset the balance of power here in Chicago."

Capone took a look at the city around us. He seemed to have a look of ownership and pride as he looked at the Wrigley Building behind me. "I'm a reasonable man," he continued. "I just want to live my life, and there's plenty of money to go around and share. But Moran is getting greedy, and I can't let the kind of bloodshed that seven masterless vampires would cause happen to my city."

"But they would have had a master. They would have had Moira." I was starting to see all the pieces falling into place.

"For a while, but as I told you before, you did me a favor by killing Moira for me. Had you not done it, I would have. So there still would have been seven vicious killers loose in our fair city."

"So you staged a massacre in order to stop a massacre?" I asked. Capone gave me another hard look, then nodded.

"Of course. This was just business and it was necessary to save the citizens of Chicago from a terrible fate. Do you know what kind of damage seven unsupervised vampires can do? Sure, with Moira dead Moran might think he could control them, but he's not one of us. Soon enough they would have been running free like a pack of wolves, killing innocent victims indiscriminately. I might be a ruthless killer, Mr. Imbierowicz, but I am a man who loves his city."

Capone hefted the package and looked at it, as if suddenly remembering that he had been holding it. He started loosening the string. "You know, Mr. Imbierowicz. I wasn't completely sure about Moira's intentions until I came back and she brought you to my house. I had really wanted to stay in Florida, but her failure to get the job done forced me to come back." He lazily dropped the string onto the snow-covered bridge deck. He started to pull off the brown paper wrapping.

"When we met, you refused a direct command from me. Most people don't live after doing that, but then again, most people don't readily ignore a command from me when I turn on my charm. You should have easily bent to my will, but you didn't. I knew then that Moira had made you. If she'd made you, then that meant she was planning to make a move against me, to free herself from my control." Capone paused from unwrapping the package and looked at me. He raised one eyebrow in a questioning expression.

Wheels and gears started turning and clicked in my head. "Are you....do you mean...no..." I stammered. "No! Don't you have to bite somebody on the neck, or something to make that happen?"

Capone laughed. The sound was loud and echoed off the bridge and buildings. "You have a lot to learn, although I don't think you'll have long to learn it. I can't have a vampire around that wasn't made by me." He continued pulling off the wrapping. "But don't worry, your family will..." Capone's voice trailed off as he pulled off the last of the paper. Underneath the paper was a stack of newspaper clippings sitting between two pieces of cardboard. Capone let the top cardboard piece fall to the ground as a shocked expression crossed his face. I could see clippings of racing forms, and on the top was scrawled a note in red ink in Agent Truesdale's distinct handwriting. "It's a sure bet that Ralphie's going down this time."

"What is this shit?" Capone's voice was menacing, with a deep guttural undertone. "Do you think this is funny? You little piece of shit!" Capone yelled as he thrust the race clippings into my face, before tossing them to the bridge with a savage jerk of his arm. Newspaper clippings swirled in the wind around our feet and blew over the railing to fall into the water of the river below. Capone's face was contorting and I could see the tips of fangs edging out from his lips. "Do you think this is a fucking joke?"

The strike was unexpected. Capone lashed out with his left fist, catching me just below my already blackened right eye. Pain shot through my face and I stumbled back. Capone followed up with a punch to my gut with his right hand that nearly doubled me over. I gasped as air exploded from my lungs. More pain came as I felt a blow to my jaw. I held up my hands to fend off the blows, which were coming faster and harder than Jack Dempsey's. I tried to lash out but I was stunned by the ferociousness of Capone's attack.

"You think this is funny?" Capone yelled. I felt a sharp pain and I could feel blood running down my neck. "You have a strange way of trying to protect your family." I then felt a tight constriction in my throat as Capone grabbed me and lifted me off the ground. He was staring up at me, his normally grey eyes now flaring with a deep red glow, like coals from a fire. He leered at me, his lips peeling back to reveal long, sharp fangs.

Damn, déjà vu. Getting choked by vampires three times in the same week does not bode well. I reached up and tried to pry Capone's fingers from my neck, but it was a feeble gesture.

"After I put you down, Mr. Imbierowicz, I will enjoy ravaging your family. They will find pieces of your father strewn about the packing plant. I'll turn him into sausage and feed him to your mother before I tear out her heart and show it to her." Capone tilted his head and smiled a grisly smile. "But I think I'll let your sister live. My brothels are always in need of fresh pussy."

I struggled and managed to hit Capone in the face, but my blow didn't phase him. *If Capone was right and Moira had made me a damn vampire, why is he so much stronger than me? Why can't I fight him?* My vision started to grey out.

Suddenly Capone flung me down, and I fell sprawling onto the cold, wet metal of the bridge. My lungs were on fire and I was bruised and battered from the beating. I looked up at Capone, gasping for breath.

"As much pleasure as it would give me to tear your throat out, your death will be much less suspicious if I shoot you. After all, you are just one more unremarkable victim of our fair city's violent culture." He reached into his coat, pulled out a small pistol from a shoulder holster, and pointed it at me. The gun might have been small, but from my perspective it looked like a cannon.

"Good-bye, Mr. Imbierowicz."

Chapter 33

I stared down the barrel of the gun, not afraid for myself, but for how I had failed my family. Capone gave me a cruel smile and winked at me as he pulled the trigger.

There was an explosion and a brilliant flash of light. The gunshot seemed to echo around the bridge. Capone jerked to the right, then was pushed backward, blood spurting from his right arm. I couldn't fully process what was happening as my own chest erupted in pain as Capone's bullet struck me. I stared, dumbfounded, as blood darkened Capone's suit jacket. Capone yelled in rage and swung his gun around, firing two more shots at me, hitting me in my chest. I collapsed in a heap onto the bridge deck, the snow cold and wet beneath me.

I heard another gunshot as Capone was hit in the shoulder. Capone turned and fired two shots toward the north end of the bridge, then he turned and ran back toward his car. My body was getting cold and numb and my vision was quickly going in and out of focus.

I looked up into the night sky, watching snowflakes fall onto me. I didn't feel any pain now, but I could feel my blood pooling under me. I closed my eyes and slowly drifted into unconsciousness.

Chapter 34

I turned in the hospital bed and looked at the man sitting in the chair. I coughed, spitting more blood onto the sheets. "That's what happened," I rasped. "I have no idea what happened from the time I went unconscious until I woke up here in the hospital. If you don't believe any of my story you can confirm it with Agents Truesdale and Wright. They know most of what happened to me."

The man sitting in the chair blew out a stream of cigarette smoke and leaned forward in his chair. "Agent Truesdale is dead. He took a bullet right between the eyes. A pretty amazing shot from over 200 feet away."

I sighed and stared up at the ceiling. *Damn.* Truesdale had been a tough son of a bitch, but he didn't deserve to go out like that.

"Agent Wright took a bullet to the head," the man continued. I shuddered, thinking the worst. "Apparently it just grazed him, but he lost a lot of blood. He managed to get to you and keep you alive until the cops arrived. He finally passed out just as they were loading you into the ambulance. He is alive, but he's unconscious right now."

My breathing became shallow, and I didn't think it was from the news about the two Federal agents. I coughed again and more blood, this time frothy, came out. "So you're saying...." My voice rasped, and I wheezed. "That all this was for nothing? No way to confirm any-thing..." Another ragged breath. "And now...(cough)... Capone gets away...(cough)...and I get to die. Hmph, it figures."

Chapter 35

The man stood up as Saul took his last breath, putting his notepad and pen into his jacket pocket. He moved to the door and opened it. "Nurse," he called. "Please get the doctor."

He turned back and stood by the door, looking at the body on the bed. After a minute the doctor came in. He moved to Saul's body and checked for a pulse, then pulled out a stethoscope and listened to the heart and lungs. A few moments later he stood up, took out a pen, and checked his watch. He made a notation on the chart while saying, "Time of death is 8:11 a.m."

The doctor turned to the man and put his pen back into his coat pocket. "What do you want us to do with the body?"

The man stepped forward into the light. He had a young, almost boyish-looking face and a penetrating gaze. He reached up and ran a hand through his dark-colored hair. "He doesn't have any family," he lied.

"Well," said the doctor, pulling out a cigarette. "I don't have anybody available right now to take the body anyway. The coroner's orderly was murdered the other night. Had his throat slashed and bled out right there in the morgue. We haven't been able to hire a replacement yet." He held out the cigarettes to the man, who took one.

The man lit the cigarette with a match. "I'll send somebody around to claim the body." He turned and headed out of the room.

Epilogue

My eyes felt like they were held shut with lead weights. I shifted slightly, my body stiff but without pain. My mind reeled with dark shapes that were filled with bright flashes and explosions of noise. Fleeting images started to come into focus, like short cuts from several different movies all jumbled together in the darkness. I saw my parents and sister arguing over dinner...Moira lifting her head back to laugh at a joke at the Green Mill...Mrs. Rabinowitz chiding me to get a second lock for my door...Bugs Moran grinning as he puffed on a cigar...Moira making love to me... and then trying to kill me...and Al Capone winking at me over the barrel of a gun as he pulled the trigger...

I awoke with a jerk. My mouth felt like it was filled with an entire bale of cotton. I blinked my eyes several times; it was like I had never opened them before. When they finally came into focus, I saw a white, corniced ceiling that was tinged yellow with cigarette smoke.

I turned my head to take in my surroundings. I was in a dimly lit room that was sparsely decorated. I lay on a couch and could make out a table sitting against the far wall. I managed to sit up, a ravaging hunger filling me. I was starving, almost as if I had never eaten in my entire life.

"Ah, I see you're awake." The voice came from my

left. I turned toward the sound and blinked as a lamp clicked on, revealing a man sitting in a dingy armchair. He was dressed in a rumpled grey suit with a white shirt and a dark blue tie, loose around his neck. He had a soft, narrow face, now covered in short stubble. His hair was black and was parted down the middle. "How are you feeling, Saul?" I recognized his voice as belonging to the man who'd interviewed me at the hospital.

I looked around and didn't recognize my surroundings. I was in an apartment, but I didn't know who lived there. "I feel fine, though I'm starving." I rubbed my head, a slight headache pounding behind my temples. My thoughts started to become clear. "Wait a minute. Didn't I die?"

"Here," the man stood up and handed me a glass filled with tomato juice and a newspaper. "These might help."

I took the glass and paper. The paper was open to page eight and I had to scan down to a small piece at the bottom of the page. "Postal employee dead in gang shoot out," read the headline. "Great," I said. "So everybody thinks I'm dead." Then a new thought struck me. "*Gevalt*! What are mom and dad going to think? And Sarah? Shit! Are they okay?"

"Your parents and sister are fine," said the man. "I have a man watching their place but, with you being dead, I don't think that Capone will make good on his threats. He's turned up back in Florida and there's no leverage for him with your family now that you are dead. Despite his many faults, Capone is not a monster."

I gave the man a look, raising one eyebrow. "Well, not a monster in the sense that he'd attack an innocent family," he said. "People would know it was him, and that would hurt his image."

I nodded and finally took a drink of the tomato juice. The sharp, coppery taste of blood filled my mouth. I spewed the drink in a violent explosion, drops raining down on the newspaper and across the room. "What the hell is this?"

"Blood."

I stared at him like he was crazy, but something inside me clicked into place. The taste had taken the edge off of my hunger. I stared at the glass and grimaced. Damn. *Or damned?* I lifted the glass again and, after a slight hesitation, took another drink, the blood flowing down my throat. I could feel my hunger becoming sated, my headache fading away. I finished the glass in three long gulps. "Do I want to know whose blood?" I asked.

"It's cows blood, actually." The man gave a sheepish smile. "I figured you wouldn't like pigs blood, being Jewish and all."

"I appreciate that. And who are you?"

"My name is Eliot Ness," he held out his hand.

I shook it and gave him a look. "So, my parents and friends think I'm dead and I've become a vampire?"

"Yep," Ness said. "That sums it up pretty well. You will be given a new name in a couple of days; you can't go around with a dead man's name. And I'm afraid you will not be able to see your family ever again." He gave me a piercing gaze. "Ever."

"But, certainly just once couldn't..."

"No." Ness shook his head. "Don't even think about it. If you showed up, it might give your poor mom a heart attack. And do you think they'd be able to keep quiet about it? You'd just be putting them right back into danger again."

I nodded slowly, realizing that he was right. I didn't like it, but I knew in my gut it was not possible. Dad might understand, and he might even be able to keep it under his hat, but if I showed up in front of mom she *would* have a heart attack. And even if she didn't, and even if she swore on my grandfather's grave, she'd never be able to keep the fact that I was still alive a secret.

I glanced around the apartment again. "Where am I? Whose place is this?"

"Yours," Ness replied. He pulled out a set of house keys and handed them to me. "This apartment happened to come into our possession a few weeks ago, so I thought it would work for you."

"What about my old place?" I asked out of curiosity. This place was clearly better than my old apartment so I really had no desire to go back.

"Well, in addition to the fact that it was *your* old apartment and you are now *dead*," Ness made it sound like it was an accusation. "We also think your old apartment is a risk. Your neighbor, Mrs. Rabinowitz, was found dead in her apartment last night."

"What?" I was shocked.

"The report that I saw said that a wild dog had broken into her apartment and attacked her. Her throat was torn out and she bled to death."

I stared at Ness, my mouth agape. She's been an old busy-body, but she hadn't deserved to be brutally killed. "But you said Capone was back in Florida. And why would he care about Mrs. R? I don't think he'd ever met her."

Ness just shrugged. He apparently didn't have any more information. I hung my head in silence for a moment, actually saying a small prayer for Mrs. R.

I looked up and walked over to the window, pulling open the heavy curtain. The bright sunlight hurt my eyes, but I think that was from not having seen it for such a long time. I looked out onto the Loop district, looking down on the sign for the Chicago Theatre. "Why are you being so nice to me?"

"Saul," Ness said, a slight smile playing across his face. "How would you like to come work for the Treasury Department?"

About the Authors

Geoff Habiger and Coy Kissee have been life-long friends since high school in Manhattan, Kansas. (The Little Apple, which was a much better place to grow up than the Big Apple, in our humble opinion.) We love reading, baseball, cats, role-playing games, comics, and board games (not necessarily in that order and sometimes the cats can be very trying). The idea for Unremarkable was sparked on a trip to Chicago and the basic idea was fleshed out on the return drive back to Kansas City. The main story, along with the characters, were fleshed out on a trip to GenCon later that year. That was over 7 years ago! But through Geoff's steadfast dedication, and Coy's staunch diligence, we managed to get Saul's story finished. Not an easy feat sometimes when we often worked long distance over Facetime.

Coy lives with his wife in Lenexa, Kansas. Geoff lives with his wife and son in Tijeras, New Mexico.

Saul's story will continue in *Untouchable*. You can also check out Geoff and Coy's fantasy crime novel, *The Wrath of the Fury Blade*.

CPSIA information can be obtained
at www.ICGtesting.com
Printed in the USA
LVOW13s0849040218
565242LV00010B/475/P